MADISON'S MIRACLES

Other books by Joye Ames:

A Time For Love
Only You
The Dowager Duchess
If Not for You
Save Your Heart for Me

Also writing as Joyce and Jim Lavene:

The *Sharyn Howard Mystery* Series

Last Dance
One Last Good-bye
The Last to Remember
Until Our Last Embrace
For the Last Time
Dreams Don't Last
Last Fires Burning
Glory's Last Victim

MADISON'S MIRACLES

•

Joye Ames

AVALON BOOKS
NEW YORK

Library of Congress Catalog Card Number: 2004100464
ISBN 0-8034-9662-1

Published by Thomas Bouregy & Co., Inc.
160 Madison Avenue, New York, NY 10016

PRINTED IN THE UNITED STATES OF AMERICA
ON ACID-FREE PAPER
BY HADDON CRAFTSMEN, BLOOMSBURG, PENNSYLVANIA

For our new grandson, Jason. May all your dreams come true!

Chapter One

Maggie Madison took hold of her courage and set a cheerful grin on her face as she knocked on the weathered wooden door. The chilly morning wind swirled through her baby-fine brown hair and reddened her cheeks. Her heart rate accelerated as she got ready to do battle. Then like a distant drum, it slowed. There was no answer.

She frowned at the sign on the door. *Fuentes and Son-Sales* glared back at her. Her lips formed a mutinous line as she raised her hand to knock again. The sound of her hand contacting the solid wooden door scared a few birds from their perches on the roof. Still no answer.

Maggie raised her hand again. This time in the form of a fist. But before she could use it, the door swung open.

An impatient face stared out at her. "Yes?"

"Good morning, Mr. Fuentes!"

Eyes the color of caramel glared at her from behind heavy, black-rimmed glasses. There was no doubt that he wasn't pleased to see her.

Adam Fuentes' face went from impatient to resigned. "Ms. Madison."

"I love the winter weather, don't you?"

"I love it when I can get my work done without interruption."

She put one brightly mittened hand on the door before he could close it against her. "Wait, please."

"I don't think we have anything to say to each other."

"You don't know what good news I have," she replied in a scolding tone. "Just this morning I found out that Mr. and Mrs. Bronstein and their daughter, Jessie, have been accepted for housing in the Brookshire development. Isn't that wonderful news?"

His expression didn't change. "What does that mean, Ms. Madison?"

"It means one more family off the street," she answered. "There's only one small hitch and the deal is done."

"Don't tell me. You need money."

Maggie smiled. "Only two hundred dollars, Mr. Fuentes. May I call you Adam? Only two hundred dollars will put the Bronstein family into their own home. What a deal, huh? Your business associates in the community have donated generously. I know you'll want to do the same."

The phone rang behind him. He glanced at it over his shoulder without moving his hand from the door. "Ms. Madison—"

"Maggie."

"Ms. Madison—"

"If you can't give the whole amount, Adam, that's fine. Whatever you can give will be a big help. I don't need to tell you how important this is to everyone. As a business member of this community, I know you'll want to donate *something.*"

He made a flying dive for the phone before it stopped ringing. The door was left unguarded. Maggie took her shot. She followed him into the dark, cramped offices of Fuentes and Son-Sales.

She ignored him as he pointed towards the open doorway while he spoke on the phone. She smiled innocently and closed the door carefully behind her. Adam frowned heavily at her, but it took more than an angry look and gesture to deter her. Especially since she'd never actually been inside The Ogre's lair.

It was a nickname Maggie and her partner, Delta, had given him. He was always scowling. The only exception was when he was telling them to leave him alone. Actually, Delta had given up trying to get him to contribute after their first encounter. He'd sent her back to the children's shelter in tears. But Maggie was made of sterner stuff. She *always* got him to contribute to the cause, no matter what it took.

She looked around his office. She'd wondered for over a year what it looked like inside. She'd joked with Delta about The Ogre keeping his father locked up, working the old man until there was nothing left of him. No one in the area could recall having met his father, yet there was the name on the sign.

Madison took off her fuzzy purple mittens. Obviously, Fuentes, the father, didn't work there. Maybe he had at one time.

The office was divided into two rooms. One looked like it was supposed to be a secretary's office. But the plain brown desk and chair were clearly unused. Stacks of paper covered the surface of the desk. Old green file cabinets flanked it. The whole room had the air of years of inactivity, yet the gray tile floors were spotless. Even the mottled green blinds on the tiny window were free of dust motes in the sunlight that pushed against them.

Intense curiosity drew Maggie into the much larger, inner office. A huge old desk squatted in the center of the room. Piles of paper were carefully organized around a good computer, the only thing that placed the office furnishings in the present day. The room reminded her of an office in a black and white detective movie from the '30's. The glass transom above the door was tilted slightly open. The metal ceiling fan spun slowly, lazily circulating warm air.

Adam was seated at the desk, glaring at her. He spoke quietly into the phone receiver and turned his back to her when he saw she wasn't going to leave. *Like he had some deep dark secret.* Maggie ignored him as she continued to explore his office.

He hung up the phone. "You're still here?"

She perched on the edge of a wooden ladder-backed chair that faced the desk and smiled at him. "Adam—"

"I don't think we need to be on a first name basis, *Ms.* Madison."

"Mr. Fuentes, then." She wrinkled her nose. "Although I think we're past the Victorian code of calling people Miss and Mr."

"Let's just cut to the chase. You need two hundred dollars this time?" He took a deep breath and faced down her cheerful smile as he got out his checkbook.

She named a figure and smiled sweetly at him. "A pretty reasonable price for everything we do for you."

"The government should send you overseas to nag other countries into doing what they want," he answered as he wrote the check. He ripped it out of the book and handed it to her before he turned away.

"That wasn't so bad, was it?" She tucked the check into her purse. "You could at least ask me *how* the Small Miracles Shelter helps keep *you* in business."

He almost laughed. She saw the beginning of a smile on his angular cheeks. A shadow of dark beard edged his full lips. Her eyes followed the contour of his brows as he looked up at her.

"I don't *want* to know why you think your shelter helps keep me in business. I just want you to leave me alone so I can get back to work."

"It's because you don't have to pay extra for insurance because the area isn't a high crime rate area," she continued as if she hadn't heard him, "and because you can feel safe working here alone. How can you put a price on that feeling of well-being?"

"Ms. Madison, why isn't it ever enough that I give to the shelter?" He sat back in his chair and put his hand over his eyes.

"You are alone, aren't you?" She glanced around the quiet office. "Does your father still work here?"

"My father?"

She nodded towards the door. "Fuentes *and Son*. I assume you're the son. Unless you're into child labor. Is your father here?"

"My father's been dead for five years," Adam explained in a softer tone. "He was a self-made man who worked his way off the streets of Mexico City. He didn't do it by getting handouts. He got up every morning and worked hard to make his life successful."

"I'm sorry for your loss." She could see that talking about his father still hurt him.

"Don't be. He lived a good life. A good, *productive* life."

Maggie didn't give up. "Surely you've known someone who just needed a little help? These aren't bad people. They need another chance."

"I gave you a check. Your big eyes and your short skirts worked like always. But don't expect me to *like* being a victim of the Madison steamroller charm."

"I can't believe you can be so hard-hearted!" Her tone suddenly lost its cool, cajoling quality as she realized what he was saying. "And I don't have big eyes or short skirts! I don't know what you think that has to do with the shelter!"

"Like you don't use that look on the other business owners and sweet talk them into doing what you want. You have every man around here *hoping* to write you a check every month!"

She was furious. She was *beyond* furious, she was *livid.* Her face was hot and her voice got steadily louder. "I haven't sweet-talked anyone! And I don't have any look I use to get help with the shelter! And women give, too!"

Adam looked satisfied with her response. "And I suppose your skirts aren't short either?"

They both looked down at her legs. Covered in purple hose and coming from beneath a green skirt, they reminded Maggie of some exotic vegetable. Sister Margaret Mary sent her home from school once for wearing a skirt that was only halfway down her thigh. But she was an adult now. She could wear what she liked.

She looked up to tell him so and found him still looking

at her legs. His gaze slowly moved up from her ankles until it reached her hemline. Her breath came a little faster. The dim office blurred around her. By the time his eyes finally reached hers, she felt lightheaded.

This was ridiculous. She must be coming down with a cold. She put a hand to her forehead but she caught herself peeking under it. Now instead of looking into his eyes, her line of vision included a wide chest and a flat stomach that narrowed down to . . .

What was she thinking? Why was she looking at him that way? He was *The Ogre.* His heart was harder than a Stone Mountain figure. She wasn't attracted to him. There was nothing attractive about him. Except maybe his eyes.

"My skirt isn't shorter than anyone else's." She rescued herself by reviving their argument. Her hand twitched, wanting to adjust her skirt. But she wouldn't give him the satisfaction! "If *you* lived in the real world, you'd know that!"

"If *you* lived in the real world," he charged, moving slowly towards her, "you'd know that charity only makes people unable to take care of themselves."

"That's not true! I help children and families get on their feet again and find places to live. They make good lives for themselves! Haven't *you* ever needed any help?"

He took another step towards her. "No, I haven't."

Maggie retreated another step. "Well if you feel that way, I won't bother you again."

He laughed quietly and took another step towards her. "Like I believe *that!*"

"And you won't have another opportunity to help your community," she said, taking another step back.

"I help where I see fit, not always where some silly girl points her manicured little finger!"

She bristled at that, holding herself erect at her full five-foot-five inches. "I don't have manicured hands. And I think these personal attacks are just to make up for your petty character!"

Adam suddenly took her hand. His grasp was determined

but gentle. She glanced at him nervously. *Was he attracted to her too?* "I—uh—"

"If you don't have anything else to say, my petty character and I would like to get back to work." He put her purple mittens in her hand.

He was standing very close to her. She could smell the faint spicy scent of aftershave. She watched as he slowly closed her fingers around her mittens. She lifted her chin and returned his uncertain stare. The wind had loosened her purple beret. Before it could slip to the floor, he caught it and patted it back on her head.

He let go of her hand awkwardly. "Sorry. I have a niece. She's always losing her gloves."

Maggie automatically put her hand up to hold the beret in place. Her fingers still tingled from his touch. "That's okay."

He smiled at her. "We're never going to agree on this."

"I know. But you're wrong."

Maggie saw his eyes narrow slightly beneath black brows. But he was still smiling. And that smile was doing strange things to her. Suddenly, he wasn't looking quite like The Ogre. She took another step back even though he didn't move.

"Good-bye, Ms. Madison."

"Good-bye, Mr. Fuentes."

"Do us both a favor and don't come back, hmm?"

Maggie's voice was a little breathless. "You'll have to come to me, if you want to donate money to the shelter!"

Adam laughed as he closed the door.

Maggie shrugged and put her mittens on her hands. She wished that she had some soap to rub on his windows. It was childish but it sounded satisfying. She stomped back down the windy side street, muttering to herself.

He'd called her a silly girl. She had degrees in family counseling and psychology. He'd never know. And the last time she had a manicure . . . well, she didn't even know if she'd *ever* had a manicure. She was angry. Like always.

Yet she kept going back. It irked her that she couldn't

get him to understand how important the shelter was to the community. She was so sure that if she could find the right words she could convince him. It was only a matter of time. But each visit ended the same way. He gave her a check but showed no interest in the shelter. She walked away, determined not to go back again. Until she walked past his office the next time and devised some other way she thought she could get past his guard.

This time was no different. Except he'd attacked her personally. He outright told her she was flirting with men to get their donations. She wouldn't be going back there again!

That wasn't the only way that it was different, a tiny, silent voice reminded her. There was that moment when she realized that he was a man and not The Ogre. It was too scary and confusing to think about. So she stuck to the facts.

Adam Fuentes kept to himself and drove a twenty-five-year-old brown Mercedes. He was a member of the Better Business Bureau and The Chamber of Commerce, though he never attended any of their functions. She knew his business had something to do with trucks. The man was a mystery.

Maggie loved a mystery. She also loved a challenge. Adam represented both. She sighed as she rounded the corner and the breeze tugged at her beret again. She knew she'd be back, knocking on his door again with a new way to convince him to give to the shelter. Before she was done, he'd beg to know everything he could about her programs. She just couldn't let it go.

The Small Miracles Shelter was only a few blocks away. With the wind at her back and her pocket full of checks, she was there in no time. The grass she'd planted last year was brown and withered with the cold. A few yellow and blue pansies struggled valiantly in the February winds. The restored 1930's house looked good with a fresh coat of paint and a new porch added during the past summer. It could legally hold up to twenty children but on some cold nights, it held more. Maggie wasn't good at turning people away.

"It's about time you got back!" Delta Sommers' broad, dark face creased into a smile. "How'd it go?"

"Great!" Maggie emptied the checks out of her jacket pockets. They scattered on the old wood table in their office.

"And The Ogre?"

"He gave. And I actually got into his office."

Delta swept her colorful scarf back across her shoulder. "He *let* you into his office?"

"Not exactly," Maggie confided. "It was more like he had to answer the phone and forgot to shut the door with me on the outside."

"You're a scream!" Delta laughed. "What did it look like in there?"

Maggie shrugged out of her jacket, put her beret and gloves on the chest beside the door. "It was really old but very clean and organized. You could eat off the floor. I think I softened him up some this time though."

"Honey, that man is like granite! He'll soften up, and so will Mount Rushmore, in about ten thousand years!"

"Well, never mind him. I think I got more than enough for the Bronsteins to move into their apartment. What's been going on here?"

Delta began to straighten out the wrinkled checks. "Dan asked us if we could take a boy from Juvvie."

"Dan, huh?"

"Don't start with me, Maggie. Officer Rogers and I don't have a blessed thing in common. You know that. This boy was put in Juvvie because he didn't have any place to go. They're looking for his parents."

"Do we have room?" Maggie helped her friend smooth out the checks.

"Do we *ever* have room?"

"No. We need a bigger house. As much as I love this one, and despite the fact that we've put so much work into it, we keep growing."

Delta counted up the amounts on the dozen or so checks. "You brought in almost two thousand dollars! Girl, you are a wonder!"

"But not as wonderful as Dan," Maggie teased.

"Maggie—"

"Maggie! Delta! Come quick! That new boy is in the bathroom with the door locked and he won't come out!"

"I'm coming, Sam," Delta told him then turned to her partner. "Never a dull moment around here!"

"Like there could be with this many kids!" Maggie put the checks into a shoebox and closed the door to the office. They would make a bank deposit later and write a check for Jessie Bronstein and her family. It was like Christmas and a birthday rolled into one happy package.

Small Miracles didn't always get involved with the entire family. They were mostly a safe house for children who would otherwise be on the street or in juvenile detention. Most of them hadn't done anything wrong. They'd either been left behind by their family or lost in the system. The shelter was their last resort.

Maggie looked at herself in the old mirror behind the door. Her shoulder-length brown hair was blown wildly on her head. She'd hoped the beret would help but her hair had simply whipped around it. Her eyes were a very common shade of blue but they seemed to be the right size for her freckle-covered nose and her generous mouth. Her Aunt Leila had always said she was thin as a rail and she supposed that description still applied to her. Lord knows when she looked down at her legs in Adam's office, they'd looked like they belonged to a rag doll.

"Toilet overflowed," Delta reported back to her. "I hope that new boy wasn't trying to flush drugs or something."

"With our plumbing?" Maggie scoffed. "We're lucky we can flush water!"

"I suppose that's true."

"Delta, do you think I'm too flirty?"

"What?" Delta looked at Maggie's face in the mirror. "You aren't flirty at all."

"Adam Fuentes said my skirts are too short and I have big eyes that I use to sweet talk people into giving money."

"Sounds like a personal problem," Delta replied. "Or maybe he's *interested*."

"Interested? In what?"

"*Who,* is correct here, honey. And who would be *you!*"

"You've got to be kidding! You should've seen the way he looked at me! I felt like a bug he was about to squash. The only thing about me that interests him is how he can get me to leave him alone."

Delta spread her large, capable hands wide. Her late husband's wedding band flashed on her left middle finger. "Well, Bug, all I know is that sometimes people are attracted to people they don't even like. It happens."

"I think if he was attracted to me, he'd want to get involved, don't you?"

"I don't know."

"Are you saying he *doesn't* like me?"

"I'm not saying anything," Delta denied. "You are sort of cute. In a stick-girl kind of way."

"Delta!"

"What? Quit looking at yourself in that mirror and wondering what The Ogre thinks about you. Come and meet the new boy."

Kevin wouldn't give them a last name. Delta told Maggie that Dan felt sure the boy was a runaway. Maybe from an abusive family. That was the way it was sometimes when a child was afraid to go back.

"Kevin, this is Maggie Madison. We run Small Miracles together."

"Hi, Kevin!"

The boy didn't look up. His clothes were torn and his face was dirty. His thick brown hair had been cut unevenly. He looked like he hadn't had a decent meal in days.

"You could say hi," Delta prompted him.

"You could leave me alone," he responded.

"We could leave you back in Juvvie," Delta added.

"Bring it on," Kevin answered flatly.

"Okay," Maggie intervened. "Let's not get into a screaming match. Kevin, we expect a certain amount of civility around here. Nothing fancy. We post chore assignments on the board by the door. We expect you to sign out if you leave and sign in when you come back. We expect you here for the night before it gets dark."

He looked up at her. "And if I'm not here?"

Delta got down to his level. "The door is locked at ten. Anyone who wants to live here better be *inside* at that point 'cause otherwise they won't be inside again."

"I'm sure we'll get along fine," Maggie said.

"I'm going out." Kevin got to his feet.

"Sign that sheet!" Delta said as the door slammed behind the boy.

"He'll catch on," Maggie told her.

"He's gonna be nothin' but trouble."

"You say that all the time."

"And most of the time, I'm right."

They made lunch for the ten kids who were there that day. The kitchen of the old house was Maggie's favorite room. The wood floors were worn but mellow with age. There was an extra wide sink and lots of counter space. Fresh fruits and vegetables were always plentiful, thanks to Mr. Garcia and his produce store. Two long tables with wide benches sat twenty kids for a meal. They'd been a handmade gift from the fire department around the corner.

It reminded Maggie of her Aunt Leila's kitchen when she'd been growing up. It had been a warm place, always full of good smells and laughter. Aunt Leila always had people stopping by for a meal and a cup of coffee. Everyone from the parish priest to the mayor of Warm Springs, Georgia had sat at her table.

"Do you ever wonder if you'll keep doing this even if you meet someone and settle down?" Delta asked, cutting tomatoes.

"I can't imagine doing anything else." Maggie stirred the macaroni and cheese in the big pot.

"But I don't know if I would've gotten involved here if

Matt were still alive. It's a big commitment of time and energy."

"Thinking about anyone special?"

Delta smiled broadly. "No. Are you?"

"No. There's no time to date," Maggie answered. "I haven't met a man I've been interested in since last year."

"Oh, yeah. That exterminator who worked on our termite problem."

Maggie grinned. "He was pretty hunky."

"Yeah. He gave us a good price on that job, too." Delta looked at her. "What happened to him?"

"He got tired of paging me and having me tell him that I was busy picking up a kid or finding a home for a kid or finding money for the house or—"

"Stop there! You're depressing me."

"Are we saying we can't have relationships with men because we're too involved with this shelter?"

"I think that's it exactly." Delta took a lot of time arranging tomato slices on a plate. "Dan asked me out today when he brought Kevin by."

Maggie stopped stirring. She knew Delta hadn't looked at another man since her husband had died of cancer three years before. "What did you say?"

"I told him that it was too soon; that I still spend a lot of time thinking about Matt and grieving for him."

"Is that true?" Maggie wished Delta would look at her.

"Sometimes," Delta replied with a sigh. "But that's what started me thinking about how demanding this place is. When would I go out with him?"

"You're off tonight," Maggie reminded her. "Are you sure you're not just making excuses for not trying again?"

"Are you trying to analyze me?"

"No. But you and Matt were married for ten years. I'd be scared to try again in case the same thing happened."

"Would you?" Delta whispered as a few kids began to file in for lunch.

Maggie shrugged. "I can't really imagine being married

to anyone for that long but if I was and I lost him, I'd be hurt and scared."

Delta nodded.

"But Matt *is* gone and you're still here. You have to move on sometime."

"I just don't know if I can do it again, Maggie. There's a piece of me that I won't ever get back again. When Matt died, I wanted to die with him."

Maggie took her hand. "But you didn't. You're here and you're young enough and healthy enough to think about another relationship."

"Well, healthy enough anyway." Delta smirked.

"And Dan is a good guy. Maybe he's a good person to get your feet wet with."

"I don't know. And what about you? Think you could ever feel anything for The Ogre besides frustration and a lust for his money? Let's say he came over and told you that you were the hottest thing since cinnamon rolls?"

"I can't picture that but I don't think so. But I did think I saw a termite again the other day!"

The two women smiled at one another in understanding then got lunch on the table.

The afternoon was hectic. There were chores to assign and papers to fill out for Kevin. They gave the check to the Bronsteins who broke down in tears when they saw it. Jessie's little face was angelic as she gave Delta and Maggie hugs and kisses. The two women were invited to a housewarming when the family got moved into the apartment.

"That's what makes it worthwhile," Delta said as the little family left the house.

"It is." Maggie wiped a tear from her eye. "But sometimes it takes so long to get there."

"I called Dan," Delta confessed as they stood at the window overlooking the busy Atlanta street.

"What did he say?"

"He's picking me up here at seven."

Maggie hugged her friend. "Good luck."

"You think it's the right thing to do?"

"Yes. Absolutely. Have a great time and don't think about me being here and dealing with the toilet that won't work."

"That's right." Delta laughed. "I have to call the plumber. I can't remember what he looked like. Was he anything like the exterminator?"

"Not exactly. *And* he has a wife and five kids."

"You know when Matt died, I'd have given anything to have been carrying his baby. You ever think about having kids, Maggie?"

"I have kids. Twenty or so of them every night."

"Your *own,*" Delta reminded her. "You know, white picket fence, handsome, understanding husband, diapers. The whole thing."

"No. There are plenty of kids already in the world. Another one would just be one more."

"You wouldn't feel that way if you met the right man."

Maggie didn't disagree, especially when The Ogre's face kept popping up in her mind.

Dan Rogers was a big, good-looking man in his mid-thirties. He wore his black hair close cropped and had a pleasant, trustworthy attitude. He'd been a cop for twelve years with the Atlanta PD.

"How's Kevin getting along?" he asked Maggie nervously while he waited for Delta.

"He'll be fine," Maggie answered although she hadn't seen anything of the boy all day. It was getting late. One curfew violation could send him back to Juvenile Detention.

"Good. That's good." Officer Rogers drew a deep breath and glanced around the room again. "You know, this never gets any easier. You'd think it would but it doesn't."

Maggie laughed. "I'm sure Delta feels the same way."

"You think?"

Delta made her entrance at that point. She smiled at Dan

then rolled her eyes at Maggie when her back was turned to him. "Page me if you need me, honey."

"You got it. Have a good time."

"We will." Dan's eyes didn't leave Delta's pretty face. "Good night, Maggie."

Maggie watched them drive away in Dan's car. She glanced up and down the sidewalks but didn't see any sign of Kevin. It was 8:45 before he walked into the shelter. He glanced defiantly at Maggie then ran up the stairs to the room he'd be sharing with three other boys. She took a deep breath, then closed and locked the shelter door for the night.

Lights out was at 10:30. Maggie watched the news on television then climbed into her own bed. A storm was raging around the city with power outages and loud thunder that rattled the windowpanes of the old house. Lightning split the sky outside her window and the night rumbled around her.

Not overly anxious about storms, she closed her eyes and settled into bed. She thought about what Delta had said about The Ogre for a few minutes. It was laughable to think that he thought of her as anything but a pest. Still, today in his office when he'd looked up at her after eyeing her legs . . .

A loud pounding at the front door made her jump. She snatched up her robe, wondering in a half-dazed fashion if Delta had forgotten her keys.

No one else was up. The kids had either slept through the disturbance or were ignoring it. Maggie ran down the stairs and opened the door. A gust of wind nearly ripped it from her hands. Rain swept in with the cold breeze but the man on the step wasn't wearing a hat or coat. His black hair was plastered to his head and his clothes were soaked to his skin. Was she still in bed dreaming or was Adam Fuentes standing on her doorstep?

Chapter Two

"Adam? Is that you?"

"Yes. I know it's late but can I come in? I need to talk to you."

Maggie wished she could even *start* to imagine why he was there. She stared at him without moving her hand from the door or giving him the idea that he should come inside. In fact, as the cold wind whipped against her again, she shivered and closed the door a little.

"This is ridiculous," he muttered and turned to walk away past the pansies that were straining for shelter against the terrible night.

"Adam? Is—is there something you wanted?" As stupid as it sounded, she was thinking about what Delta had said to her earlier. *Was he there because he was attracted to her?* Hadn't she just been thinking about it in bed? She swallowed hard and her heart beat a little faster.

"I'm here because I'm a fool. I've come all this way and I don't know what to say to you. Good night."

Maggie shivered again and pulled her robe closer. This had to be a dream. It wasn't really happening. The Ogre wasn't *really* interested in her. This had to be her subconscious and late night pizza talking.

But what if he was attracted to her? What would she say? She'd never thought of him that way. At least not until today in his office. And even then it wasn't anything serious. This was awkward. What should she say? "Maybe we can talk tomorrow?"

He seemed to change his mind suddenly. He turned around and came stalking back up to where she stood in the doorway. "Tomorrow might be too late. I know you don't owe me anything. I know I've given you a hard time. But if you have a minute—"

Her eyes opened wide on his good-looking, rain-soaked face. The growth of dark beard was attractive in a virile, masculine way that made her stomach muscles tighten. The dark tie he'd been wearing earlier in the day was gone. The rain had soaked his white shirt to his chest. Her toes started tingling. She groaned and shook her head. It was a sure sign that, despite everything, she *was* attracted to him.

Delta was right. Not only did he want her, he wanted her right now, at that moment! He'd walked through the storm to see her because it couldn't wait until morning. She couldn't think of anything to say to him. She held the door open and watched as he walked into the kitchen.

He stood there, dripping rain on her wood floor. "Thanks, Maggie."

The scent of the stormy night swirled around her. It was tinged with the faint spicy aftershave she remembered from that afternoon. She closed the door behind them, bustling around the kitchen. *Anything not to be so aware of him.* She grabbed a yellow towel from the laundry room and handed it to him.

"Would you like some coffee?" She looked away from him, disturbed by his nearness. Her thoughts were unfocused like the storm outside. She had to get a grip.

"If you have it, that would be good. Thanks. I've been walking the streets for hours."

"We always keep a pot on. Sometimes they bring kids to us during the night and we all need a cup to fill out the paperwork."

"I'm sorry about your floor." Adam put the towel down on the puddle he'd created.

"That's okay. It's had worse done to it." Maggie poured

coffee into two happy face mugs. The fragrant brew was real enough to make the situation even more *un*real. She hadn't felt this way since she was a teenager. Her palms were sweaty and her knees were shaky. She took a seat at one of the wood tables and waited for him to do the same. All the time her mind was racing. *What was she going to say to him?*

"I'm sorry to come to you this way," he said as he took his seat opposite her. "I didn't know what else to do."

"You—uh—didn't?"

"No. Once I realized what happened, I knew I had to do something. I had to tell someone."

Maggie cleared her throat. Dreamworld time was over. This was really happening. She didn't really even know Adam besides their little skirmishes every month. Maybe if they spent some time together or could find some common ground . . .

What was she thinking? This was The Ogre. "I realize that sometimes these things come on strong and fast, Adam. You don't expect it. It's happened to me before, too."

"It has?"

"Yes. And it's nothing to be ashamed of." She used her best clinical voice. She hoped he didn't notice that it sounded kind of wispy.

"Ashamed?"

"Yes. We don't know each other very well. But people can be attracted to people very strongly from very little contact."

"*What?*"

Maggie glanced up at his surprised face. Her heart was beating so hard in her chest it felt like a brass band. "You *did* walk through the storm to talk to me."

"About my *niece*," he answered, getting to his feet. "I'm sorry. I didn't realize that you had feelings for me! I—"

"No! Not *me*! I thought *you*—"

"Not *me*!"

"Oh! My mistake. Sorry."

"That's okay." He glanced around the big kitchen uncomfortably. *What am I doing here anyway?*

Maggie swallowed hard. "Please sit down and tell me about your niece."

The words came out of her mouth as her professional demeanor dropped into place. Inside she cringed. How could she be so stupid as to think The Ogre was attracted to her? When she saw Delta, she was going to hit her for putting such stupid thoughts into her head. Then she was going to hit herself for thinking them!

Adam took his seat but he looked at her warily. It was uncanny. Maggie Madison had been The Annoyance for so long that he hadn't really thought of her as an attractive woman—until that afternoon at his office. When she suddenly accused him of coming there to hit on her, his mind flashed back to her long legs and that silly little skirt she wore. When she leaned over, he could almost see her—

"It was an easy mistake to make." Adam shifted uneasily on the hard bench. She was an attractive woman. Not his type, maybe. Not that he had a type. He'd almost forgotten was dating was.

"Please." Maggie held up her hand. "It was nothing. The product of waking up out of a deep sleep."

He glanced at his watch. "You must go to bed early. It's barely ten forty-five."

"Never mind. You were going to tell me about your niece?"

"Jordan." He drew a deep breath. "My niece, Jordan, ran away earlier this evening. I found a note on her bed. The police said they couldn't promise anything about finding her. They said so many kids run away, they can't find all of them. They said that you might be able to help me."

Maggie looked at the damp, crumpled note he put on the table in front of her. "How old is Jordan?"

"She just turned thirteen."

"And you've had problems with her before?"

"Not really. Her mother and father were killed in a car accident last year. She's been living with me since it happened. We don't have any other family. She was kind of shell-shocked to begin with. I thought she was getting over it. Then we started having some problems the last few months."

"What kind of problems?"

"She doesn't want to go to school. She won't come home on time. We get into arguments about her clothes and her friends. I never claimed to be her father. I know I can't replace my brother. I've never even been married." His voice was vehement and his eyes were fierce. "I just didn't want a stranger to raise her."

Maggie shivered with something her professional demeanor couldn't protect her from and looked away. She grabbed a piece of paper and a pen to cover her confusion. What was wrong with her anyway? She hoped she wasn't coming down with a cold. "Why?"

Adam looked puzzled. "Why . . . what?"

"Why don't you think of yourself as Jordan's father figure? If you're all she has, that's exactly what you are in her life. You have the right to question her lifestyle. You just have to relax, stop worrying about it. She needs you to help her make decisions. Especially right now when she might not be thinking clearly."

He sat up straighter on the bench, as though fending off her attack on his words. "I knew I should've sent her away to school. Someone else might know how to deal with her. I work a lot of hours. And I don't know anything about raising a teenager."

"How does Jordan feel about that?"

He ran his hand across his face. "Who can tell? We don't talk anymore. I don't know what she wants to do. But I think she must be pretty unhappy to do something like this."

Maggie studied the note. It was written in a childish scrawl with an orange crayon. There were no demands or explanations. *"I'm leaving to live with some friends. Don't bother to look for me. I don't want to be any more trouble or make you miss any work. Jordan."*

"What do you think?" he asked finally when she didn't say anything.

"I think she needs counseling. You probably both do. Jordan has issues that aren't being resolved. I'm sure her parents' deaths were hard on both of you. Sometimes it seems like you're taking it all right. But inside, you keep asking the big questions. It takes time and patience to get over something like this. In the meantime, the two of you are going to have to work on learning to be a family."

Adam couldn't disagree. It was easy to talk to Maggie. She had a very soothing voice and an engaging manner. He wasn't sure how he'd missed it all that time. When he put all of her together, it was no wonder his colleagues contributed to her cause so easily. "We can't do that if she's gone. Can you find her?"

"I don't know. She could be anywhere by now."

"Is that it? Is that the best you can do?"

"What do you want me to say, Adam? The police were right. Hundreds of children run away every day, in every city in this country. Finding them is tough unless they're picked up for a crime."

He shot to his feet. "So why did the police send me to you?"

She got up slowly and tucked her pink bunny robe around her with as much dignity as she could muster. "Because I can *probably* find her. The chances are she hasn't gone far yet. I have some connections. I'll do what I can. Do you have a picture of her?"

He took a school photo out of his pocket. "So, what do we do now?"

Maggie studied the photo. The girl looked a lot like her uncle. The same light eyes, dark complexion and black hair. "I'll check with my local connections. Spend some time on the streets. Ask if anyone's seen her. Sometimes you get lucky. I can't promise anything but I'll do the best I can."

"Okay. Let's go."

"I can't just leave the shelter. Someone has to be here.

It's part of our license. The kids can't be left without supervision at night."

"I'll pay you."

"I'm not a private detective. And I have too much invested here to give it up to look for one child."

"Look—"

"No, *you* look—"

The door burst open. Rain and cold air swept into the kitchen along with the scent of wet pavement. Delta and Dan were laughing as they ran into the shelter. Both of them were soaked but neither seemed to notice. They had eyes only for each other and didn't see Maggie or Adam.

"Delta?" Maggie tried to get her friend's attention.

"Maggie? What are you doing up? Is something wrong? Did they bring us another one, knowing we're already over quota?"

"Adam Fuentes' niece ran away today."

Delta frowned, marring her pretty face. "The Ogre? And I suppose he wanted our help? That man's got a lot of nerve!"

"He should go to the police," Dan included.

"He *did* go to the police." Adam got to his feet. "They said I should come here and talk to the women at the shelter because they know the area."

Maggie shrugged when Delta glared at her. It wasn't her fault that she didn't notice him.

"Mr. Fuentes." Dan shook his hand. "I'm Officer Rogers, Atlanta PD. I'm sorry for your trouble. I'm sure if anyone can find your niece, Maggie and Delta can."

"I'm sorry, too, Mr. Fuentes. I'm Delta Sommers. I work here with Maggie." She took his hand. "I didn't recognize you."

"I remember you, Ms. Sommers." He glanced at Maggie. "Can we go now?"

Everyone looked at her. Maggie felt trapped. "I'll have to get dressed. And we'll have to decide which way to go."

"What's wrong?" Delta followed Maggie up the stairs,

leaving the two men in the kitchen. "You don't usually drag your feet when there's a child to find."

"I don't know. It's his attitude. He offered to pay me to leave the shelter to look for his niece."

"People are distraught when their children run away. You know that. I guess he's not any different."

"*You* were dressed. You didn't have to volunteer me," Maggie pointed out as she scrounged around for a pair of jeans and a sweater in her bedroom. "*You* could've gone out with him."

"You're just in a bad mood. It was your idea for me to spend some quality time with Dan. It's not *that* late yet! I think we can find some more *quality*."

Maggie pulled on a pair of old boots and ran a brush through her hair. "I feel sorry for him. It's just . . . weird."

Delta nodded and grinned at her. "He likes you, honey. I can tell."

"Don't start!"

"What? You want me to fall in love and have to juggle this place with a normal life. What about you?"

"I made an idiot out of myself when he first came in tonight." Maggie frowned at her. "I pretty much told him I thought he was here to hit on me."

"No!"

"Yes!" Maggie picked up her coat. "And it's your fault!"

"My fault? I wasn't over there flirting with the man today."

"Delta!"

"I'm just kidding." Delta put her hands on Maggie's shoulders. "Why are you so sensitive about it? You didn't mind me joking about the exterminator."

"I told you. He said I use my big eyes and short skirts to sweet talk people out of money. How do you expect me to feel?"

"The man needs our help. Maybe this is a good time to reform The Ogre, huh?"

"Why don't *you* reform him then?"

"I'd say because he likes your skinny legs and stick

body, honey." Delta laughed at her. "Dan and I will keep the place quiet while you're gone."

"I'm so sure."

Maggie pulled a waterproof poncho over her purple coat. She glared at her friend one last time then walked slowly down the stairs in the silent house. The storm had mostly subsided. There was some rumbling in the distance but the worst had passed them. One of the kids got up and headed for the bathroom. The old pipes creaked and groaned, then there was the sound of gushing water.

"Oh no." Delta groaned with them.

"Oh-oh. I hope Dan knows something about plumbing."

"You evil woman," Delta whispered as they entered the kitchen.

"Why should I have all the fun?"

Adam looked at Maggie in her bright orange poncho with parts of the deep purple coat showing through on the sleeves and neck. Neither garment went much past her thighs but now those limbs were encased in worn blue jeans. The woman was a walking fashion disaster. But there was something about those long legs and that delicate face under the wispy hair that made him want to—

Maggie grabbed a flashlight from the wall near the door and, interrupting his thoughts, said, "Let's go."

Adam nodded and tried to collect his rambling thoughts. One way or another, the woman drove him crazy.

Dan clapped him on the shoulder. "Good luck, Adam."

"Thanks, Dan." The two men shook hands then Adam ran down the stairs after Maggie. "Wait a minute," he called after her when she showed no sign of slowing down.

Maggie reluctantly slowed her strides for him to catch up with her. It would've been much easier to look for Jordan without his help.

"Do you have any idea where to look for Jordan?"

"I must have or you wouldn't be here," she countered sarcastically.

"Look, I know we don't always get along—"

"I think that's hardly the case." She started to walk double time again down the dark, wet sidewalk. "We *never* get along. You said terrible things to me this morning."

"I'm sorry if I got personal. But I still don't believe that people need charity. They need jobs and the will to get up every morning."

"Well, that must not always be the case because here we are."

"I offered to pay you."

"I told you, I'm not a private detective. You couldn't pay me to do this for you."

"Then why—?"

"Because it's important." She slogged by him. "Because it matters to these kids that there's someone who cares about them."

"Then what *do* you want?"

She sighed. "A house big enough that I don't have to break the rules by letting kids stay there at night. Parents who put their kids first. And peace on earth. How about you?"

He shoved his hands into his pockets to protect them from the biting wind. "Are you always so sarcastic?"

"I guess it's my way of coping with what I do."

"If you have to cope, why do it? Why not do something with fewer problems?"

Maggie studied his face in the streetlight's glare. "Because someone was there when I needed them to be there for me. But not everyone has an aunt they can go to when their parents don't want them."

Adam was silent for a long time as they walked. "You were abandoned?"

She was sorry she'd said anything but it was too late. As usual, her mouth had gone on without her brain. "My mother died. My father was a musician who needed to go on the road for his career. He decided that he needed to go *without* his daughter."

"I'm sorry," Adam muttered, feeling like a fool. "I didn't know."

"How could you?" She sighed and hunched her shoulders

down into her poncho for warmth. "But that's the way it is with these kids. They all have a story. They all need someone. I was lucky. I meet hundreds of kids every year who don't have anyone to take them in and they end up on the street."

"And you're that someone?"

"Right now." She watched as a raggedy man fished for food in a dumpster behind a convenience store.

"It must be hard on your husband." The words were out before Adam could call them back. *Idiot! Could I be any more obvious?*

Maggie tossed him a sidelong glance. "Even if I met Prince Charming, there wouldn't be time to date him."

"That's what Vickie said about me. I guess I wasn't very good at juggling my personal and professional life."

"Is Vickie your ex-wife?" she wondered in a loud voice as a garbage truck passed them on the street.

"No. I've never been married. Six months was a record for me having a relationship."

Maggie waited until the street was quiet again. "Are you any better now? I mean, have you thought about getting married for Jordan's sake? Another woman could make a big difference in her life."

"I guess not. I caught that crack Jordan made in her note about me working. She doesn't understand what it takes to survive. And I wouldn't get married for Jordan's sake. We have enough problems with just the two of us." He looked around at the deserted back street. "Where are we going anyway?"

Maggie took a deep breath and reminded herself that she wasn't with the hunky exterminator who Delta loved to tease her about. This was Adam Fuentes, The Ogre. Not some nice man with a great smile and fabulous eyes. His voice wasn't supposed to make her heart do flips. "I know a shelter about a mile from here. We'll start there."

"We could've taken the car."

"But then we might have missed something," she educated him. "Street kids hang out at night. Even in bad weather. We'll be walking under the interstate bypass bridge. It's a popular place."

The rain had stopped but the night was still misty. It was like a cold, wet blanket covering the city. The mist hovered around the streetlights, making a halo of the moisture. The wind crystallized their breaths in the darkness as they walked.

"How long have you been doing this?" Adam wished he could ease the tension between them.

"About five years."

"You don't look old enough."

"I'm twenty-six." Was he trying to get information from her? "I started working in a shelter when I got out of high school and wrote my college thesis on street life."

"You must've been very dedicated." He pursued the subject as he followed her.

"I knew what I wanted to do," she answered. "It was important to me. It will always be important to me."

"So you've given up on having a life of your own before you ever had one. That's dedication."

"Not that it matters," she informed him tersely, "but I have a life. And I'm very happy with it."

He smiled at her, enjoying the way the mist glistened on her face and lips. "I guess that's how you got so determined in your cause?"

"Is that a nice way of saying I'm a pain in the butt?"

"I know you mean well, Maggie. And I know there are kids out here that need your help. But your fundraising techniques leave a lot to be desired."

They stopped to argue beneath a lighted green overhang from a small Chinese market. Adam's black hair was wreathed in mist. Maggie looked into his eyes as he spoke. For a moment, she was lost in his words and the sound of his voice.

A man on a bicycle passed them on the sidewalk, swerving close to her. Adam moved between them. His long fingers curled protectively around her arm. She could feel his touch through her sweater, warm and reassuring.

"What I don't get is an educated man like yourself not understanding why the shelter is so important." Her voice was a little breathless to her ears.

"What do you mean?"

"You're intelligent. Well-off. Self made." *Sexy eyes. Nice shoulders. Great voice.*

"Stop! You'll ruin my *Ogre* reputation!"

She looked away. "Delta didn't mean anything by that. She didn't realize who you were."

"I guessed that. Do you have a dartboard with my picture on it in your office?"

"Contrary to your beliefs, I don't spend all my time thinking about you."

"No," he agreed. "Just my money."

"Only the part that you aren't giving me," she quibbled.

"If you're so hot for my money, why didn't you take me up on my offer when I tried to pay you?"

"There's a difference," Maggie assured him. "I don't expect you to understand."

"Try me," he suggested as the rain started falling steadily again. "You might be surprised."

"All right. Collecting money for what the kids need is one thing. Taking money from a miserable parent or guardian is another. I don't make money on people's problems."

He considered her words. "Except that if there weren't any unhappy families in the world, you wouldn't have the shelter."

"I'm ready to be out of business any time the world is ready to make people better parents."

"Is that what I am?" he asked her seriously. "A bad parent?"

Maggie looked at him. A feeling of closeness was developing between them. It was only an illusion. It was the night and the mist that made him seem different. He was still Adam Fuentes, the man she'd feuded with for a year.

"Shh," she cautioned, avoiding an answer to his question. "I see a few kids. We don't want to scare them off. They might think we're cops."

He squinted through the mist. "Who might? I don't see anyone."

Maggie pointed towards the dark, looming shape of the bridge. Traffic streamed by overhead. Red and white lights flashed as Atlanta commuters braved the raw night. Just underneath was a flickering orange light and a small amount of smoke. A group of people stood around a fire that burned in an old washtub.

"Let me do the talking," she warned. "They know me."

Adam nodded, not trusting his voice anyway. He could see as they approached the group that most of them were children. The youngest one wasn't more than eight or nine. The older ones looked like teenagers. He shuddered in the cold. Jordan could be out in the night with a group of people like this one.

"Hey, bad night, huh?" Maggie approached them.

"We ain't done nothin'," one of the older boys proclaimed.

"I didn't say you did. I'm Maggie Madison."

Another boy nodded. "I know you. You're from the shelter."

"That's me. You usually hang out at Wendwood?" She named the other local shelter.

"Nah. Shelters is for babies." The two boys slapped hands over the dying fire.

Maggie ignored their remark. She heard it all the time. "We're looking for a girl."

A few of the older boys made some crude remarks. Sparks from the fire flew into the damp air and died.

"What's this girl look like?" one of them asked.

"Do you have the picture?" Maggie turned to Adam.

"Yes." He pulled Jordan's photo from his jacket pocket.

"This is her." Maggie didn't listen to the base remarks and loud whistles from the boys. She held out the picture for them to see in the firelight.

"What's she done?" the first boy asked.

Maggie bluffed. "She's sick and she doesn't have any medicine."

"Maybe she just wanna let it go," the second boy suggested. He looked at Adam. "You her Daddy?"

"Yes," he lied. He didn't have to tell them his life story. "Have you seen her?"

The boy looked him over carefully. "Maybe. What's in it for me?"

"A hundred dollars if you can take me to her."

The two boys looked at each other. "We can do it!"

"Adam," Maggie whispered, "I'm supposed to do the talking, remember?"

"I think I can handle it from here," he replied, feeling that he understood the boys.

"This isn't like doing business with adults," she argued. "You shouldn't have flashed that money."

"Just because you're not motivated by money for yourself doesn't mean the rest of the world isn't." He started to walk away, following the boys who offered to take him to Jordan. "Thanks for your help, Maggie."

"Wait!" she cautioned. "You can't trust them."

The fog was coming in thick and wet. Adam disappeared into it with the two boys. Maggie ground her teeth then turned away. She wasn't following after him. He'd asked for her help. She'd given it. If he wouldn't listen, that was his problem. He'd find out how it worked soon enough.

Chapter Three

Maggie convinced one of the younger girls to come back with her to the shelter. The girl's name was Jasmine but she liked to be called Jazzy. She told Maggie that she'd seen Jordan at the mall that day.

Jazzy looked around the shelter when they got there and tucked her dark, damp hair behind her ears. "Nice place. How many kids you got here?"

"Too many." Maggie closed the door. "But I think we can find one more bed for the night. We'll see what we can do tomorrow."

Delta always kept a spare cot in a closet upstairs. It was small but could fit in any of the rooms. Maggie found Jazzy some dry clothes and laid out the bed. She dug out some blankets for the child. She looked at the sleeping faces of the other girls in the room and sighed. Sometimes it broke her heart to think these children might never reclaim their parents. What she and Delta did was important but it would never be the same as a family to these kids.

"Goodnight," she whispered to Jazzy. She restrained herself from kissing the girl's cheek and reassuring her again. Most of the kids there had been hurt too badly to easily accept affection from strangers. It took time and patience to gain their trust. They took meals and a warm place to sleep, even clothes or money, but they didn't believe that anyone could love them if their parents didn't care.

She'd felt the same way for many years growing up with her aunt. Not that Aunt Leila didn't love her and didn't show her every kindness. But her father didn't care about her or he would've stayed. To her young mind, even her mother who'd died had left her behind. Why would anyone else care about her if they didn't?

Maggie closed the door behind her and made her way back downstairs. She was wet and cold and wanted one more cup of coffee before turning in for the night. She wondered how far that hundred dollars would get Adam in his quest to find his niece. The information Jazzy gave her was more likely to be trustworthy. The kids banded together for the most part; they didn't give each other up easily. But that wouldn't keep those two boys from taking Adam on a trip he wouldn't soon forget!

She shivered again as she poured some coffee and added milk. There was a small light on in the living room, the only place with formal furniture in the house. They used it mainly to meet with local supporters or when a child's parent came to claim him or her. Maggie wandered back that way and reached to turn on the light when she heard a noise in the darkness. "Who's there?"

There was a startled gasp then a hasty movement. Maggie saw a flash of Delta's face in the dim light and heard Dan's deep voice.

"Maggie?"

"Delta? I brought in another kid for the night."

"Honey, we're three over occupancy now," her friend reminded her.

"And I'm not listening to this conversation," Dan added. "I'm an officer of the law, you know? If you two are going to do things that aren't legal, don't let me know about them."

Delta drawled, "Oh, Dan. You wouldn't report us, would you?"

"Not if I don't know about it, angel."

Maggie heard something that sounded like a quick kiss then Dan muttered something about having to be on duty in the morning.

Delta walked him to the back door. Maggie shuffled behind, giving them a few moments of privacy.

When he was gone and they were alone, Maggie smiled at her friend. "I guess it went pretty well, huh?"

Delta leaned against the door and sighed. Her brown eyes were bright and misty. "Oh, honey, it was better than that. It was . . . wonderful."

Maggie washed out her coffee cup and put it on the side of the sink. "It sounded like it."

"Sounded like it?"

"All that muffled groaning and smooching."

Delta laughed. "Just because your man took you out on the street—"

"He's not *my man.*"

"Oh, sorry. He hasn't made his move yet?"

"No. And he's not going to! Stop saying things like that. We barely tolerate each other. There's nothing romantic between us."

"Okay, honey. Don't get your engines all revved. What about his niece?"

"We walked down to the bridge. Adam offered some boys a hundred dollars to help him find her."

Delta groaned. "Oh, no! Couldn't you stop him?"

"He just left with them after brushing me off with a polite thank you. I think it was to prove that money can buy anything he needs."

"No wonder he doesn't like to part with any of it then!"

Maggie yawned. "I'm not going to worry about him. He's a big boy. I'm sure he can take care of himself."

"He'll be back. That hundred dollars was wasted."

"It would be better if he didn't come back," Maggie told her bluntly. "He and I are like oil and water."

"Chalk and cheese?"

"Exactly."

"Vinegar and peanut butter?"

"Good night, Delta."

Maggie slept late the next morning. It was Delta's turn to make breakfast for the house full of kids. Because she planned on going out to the Starlight Mall that day, she wore warm blue tights and a red wool dress. She looked at the hemline that grazed her mid-thigh and shrugged. She wasn't going to let Adam or anyone else make her feel uncomfortable about the way she dressed.

She ran a brush through her fine hair and applied some gloss to her chapped lips. The cold weather wreaked havoc on her face when she was out at night. It seemed logical that the rain would act to moisturize, but it never worked that way for her. She didn't waste time with blush or eye makeup. Her eyelashes were naturally dark and her cheeks were always pink. She zipped on knee high black boots and skipped downstairs.

The smell of Delta's homemade waffles had been taunting Maggie's stomach since the first load of kids left for school that morning at six. It gave a sharp grumble as she entered the warm kitchen.

"You missed the rush, Sleeping Beauty," Delta greeted her. "Waffle?"

"Thanks." Maggie sniffed the golden circles appreciatively.

Delta used her spatula to point at the table. "I guess she's your new girl?"

"Jasmine. Jazzy. She said she was thirteen but I think she might be nine or ten."

"And I think *that*'s your good deed over there." Delta used the utensil to point to the second table. "He was out here on the stoop when I came down this morning. He's looking pretty pathetic."

Maggie glanced at Adam. He was a mess, playing with some coffee in his cup and ignoring the waffle on his plate. His clothes were dirty and torn and he had a scratch on the side of his face.

"Hey, Mister," the boy beside him said, "can I eat that if you're not gonna?"

Adam looked at the plate. "What? Oh. Sure."

"Thanks." The boy moved closer and whispered, "I hear you're looking for your niece on the street."

"That's right."

"I might know where you can find her."

"You do?" Adam's voice was hopeful.

"For fifty bucks, I can find anyone," the boy asserted.

Adam's expression turned skeptical. "Really?"

"More coffee?" Maggie asked, intervening. "Ed, I think it's time for you to go to school."

Ed groaned but he slid off the bench and went to get ready to leave.

Adam looked up at her. "Is there an 'I told you so' in that pot with the coffee?"

Maggie studied his tired, dirty face and disheveled hair. "I don't think so."

She poured them both a cup of coffee and put her plate down on the table beside his.

"Why not? I thought for sure you'd gloat over this."

Maggie couldn't believe it. "I hope I'm not that shallow. Besides, you didn't know any better. What happened?"

"I think we walked through most of downtown and explored every dumpster and all-night coffee shop and pool hall along the way."

"How much did it end up costing you?" She felt sorry for him despite the fact that he ignored her warning. She understood how anxious he was to find his niece.

"Probably three hundred dollars." In his eagerness to find Jordan, he didn't count the cost of every game of pool, every soda, and every pizza the boys asked for during the night. They abandoned him about three miles from the shelter. He found his way back with the help of a police officer who saw him wandering the street. It was embarrassing to admit how stupid he'd been to go with them. But not so bad that he couldn't admit that he was wrong and ask for Maggie's help again.

"Then you've paid your dues, Adam," Maggie said. "Now, if you're ready to quit playing around, let's see if we can find your niece."

* * *

They were going to Adam's condo about a mile away. She wanted to take a look around Jordan's bedroom. With any luck, she might get some clues about where to look for the girl. Maggie started her sturdy, dependable, eight-year-old Toyota. She saw Adam look at the ancient, decaying vehicle with something akin to fear in his eyes. "What's wrong? Your Mercedes is older than this!"

He climbed carefully into the passenger seat. "How do you know that?"

"I don't know," she mumbled, feeling silly that she'd gathered details about him. "Someone pointed you out to me while you were in it, I think."

"Anyway, it's not how old the car is," he replied quietly. "A Mercedes is built better. It ages. It doesn't fall apart."

Maggie gunned the Toyota's engine as she turned out of the side street to the main road. "You're a snob, Adam."

"Because I prefer quality?"

"Because you think an eight-year-old Toyota isn't as good as a twenty-five-year-old Mercedes. And because you really thought you could buy yourself out of that spot last night. You thought your hundred dollars was better than my appeal to the boys' better natures."

"Those boys don't have better natures," he declared. "And if I'm a snob, that must make you a dreamer."

"I've had people say worse."

"I'm sure."

"Like that I use my short skirts and big eyes to get money out of people." She kept her eyes on the road. "Or that I sweet talk people into doing what I want."

He studied her profile as she negotiated a lane change. Her delicate features masked the strength and courage of a tiger. "I'm surprised my opinion of you makes any difference."

She snorted. "It doesn't make any difference! I was explaining that people have said worse things about me. Funny how both of those things came from you, isn't it? And yet here I am, helping you find your niece."

He saw her push impatiently at her flyaway hair. She

wrinkled her nose at herself in the rearview mirror. Something warm and reluctant gave way inside of him. "I appreciate you helping me with Jordan *despite* our previous relationship, Maggie."

She smiled at him when he said her name then shook her head. *Stick to business!* "Why did you give that money to the boys last night?"

"Your argument didn't seem very convincing. They didn't act like they were going to help."

"So you thought your money would appeal to their baser sides and they'd help you? That doesn't make any sense."

He sighed. "I wasn't looking at it sensibly, I guess. I just wanted to find Jordan."

Maggie impulsively covered his hand with hers. "We'll find her. Jazzy had no reason to lie to me about seeing her at the mall. I think we'll find her there."

Adam looked at her slender, pale hand on top of his darker, larger one. Her touch was cool and light but he could feel the impact of it through the length of his body. "Why are *you* doing this?"

Self-consciously, Maggie removed her hand and put it back on the steering wheel. She would've touched anyone else, it wasn't anything special. "I guess I'm just a people person. Delta says I hug a lot too."

"I don't mean *that,*" he began, sorry that her hand was gone. "I mean the whole thing. I've hurt your feelings. We've never had a civil conversation. Why are you helping me find Jordan?"

"It's what I do. Take the girl I picked up last night. Jazzy's parents dropped her off to fend for herself. They didn't have jobs and felt like someone else should care for her. Do you have any idea what that does to a child? They don't just need clothes and a place to get off the street. They need counseling and a feeling that they're not so much trash to be left behind when times get rough."

"I know you're very passionate about it," he observed. "I didn't mean to say—"

"Never mind. You're not the first to say it," she muttered darkly. "Or the first person who didn't understand."

"I didn't say I don't understand."

"It doesn't matter."

"I can see we're never going to agree on anything."

"You're probably right. But we agree that Jordan should be home."

"That's true. This is it." He pointed to the large group of condominiums on the right. "Thanks for the lift home. I just started walking last night, hoping I'd find her. Then I ended up at your place."

Maggie pulled the car into the parking garage of the expensive brick homes. She couldn't help recalling how lost and vulnerable he'd looked when she opened the door last night. It wasn't good for her to think of him that way. Her emotions were still a little confused about him.

Adam smiled uneasily as she parked beside his brown Mercedes. "It'll just take me a minute to change. We can take my car from here."

"That's fine." She got out and walked around the car.

"You don't have to come up," he insisted as she stood beside him.

"I suppose I wouldn't have to," she returned. "I could just sit down here and choke on the carbon monoxide fumes."

He took a deep breath as the elevator doors opened. *Patience.* "Of course, you're welcome to come up and wait."

Maggie smiled warmly and stepped into the elevator beside him. "I might be able to get some ideas about where to look for Jordan from her stuff."

"I thought you said she was at the mall?"

"She's not *living* at the mall. She's just hanging out there. And if she's not there today, we want to know where she's spending the night. She's got to be staying with a friend." Adam was clearly as uncomfortable with her as she was with him. Good, she wanted to shake him up a little. The man was way too smug and self-assured about his opinions being right.

She glanced at him in the elevator as he pressed the buttons to go up. He was in his own little world. His tight illusion of control didn't exist. What must it do to a man like him to have his niece run away and not be able to find her? Probably the most important question would be: what would he do when he finds her? "I'm surprised you didn't hire a private detective."

"I wanted to keep this quiet. For Jordan's sake as well as my own."

Maggie wasn't fooled. "You mean you're embarrassed to admit you lost control of the situation."

"Are you always this perceptive with everyone or am I a special case?"

She looked into his beautiful eyes and swallowed hard. *There was that feeling again.* The elevator was much smaller than she first noticed. Why was it so warm? She ignored the sudden urge to tug down on her skirt. Everything seemed wrong. She wished that she'd waited in the car.

A chime sounded softly and the doors opened. Maggie took a deep breath as though she'd been underwater for too long and walked quickly into the hallway.

Adam held the elevator door for her and took out his key. "After you. Third door down and to the right."

"Thanks." She was acutely aware of him following behind her. She supposed he was looking at her legs, thinking they were too long and too skinny. Or condemning her because her skirt was too short. At least he couldn't accuse her of trying to get money from him this time.

She walked right past the third door, lost in her thoughts about him. She reached the window at the end of the hall and looked back at him.

He was waiting at the door to his apartment. Expressive eyes moved slowly over her. "It's here."

"You could have said something," she complained as she marched back towards him.

"Sorry." He couldn't believe that he was watching her

walk like some mesmerized schoolboy. What was wrong with him? "I wasn't paying attention."

"I suppose you were gloating because I can be wrong, too?"

Adam unlocked the door. "I wasn't gloating. I was watching you."

Maggie felt warmth flood her cheeks. She swept past him into the apartment with the barest glance at the entryway. "If you're about to make another crack about my skirt being too short, don't bother."

Adam dropped his keys into a blue glass bowl. He took off his jacket and left it on a table near the door. "Look, if I apologize for saying that about your skirts, could we forget I said it and call a truce?"

She faced him with her chin held high. "I think it's always best to be honest, even if it's not what we want to hear."

"Then, honestly," he continued, "I was having a bad day when you came in yesterday. You have an excellent reputation. I just think people should work for what they want. *Adult* people. I've known too many people who lost their ability to succeed through the kindness of people like you."

"Not everyone is like that."

"I'm finding that out."

If he wasn't watching me to berate me . . . Maggie glanced avidly at his apartment to cover her immediate confusion. She didn't want to know why he was watching her. It was bad enough knowing that he was in the first place. Suddenly, she felt awkward and uncertain. Delta's words kept playing over and over in her mind. *He likes you.*

The condo was like him, subdued and a little stiff. The sand-colored furniture didn't look like anyone ever sat on it. She felt certain a drink was never spilled on the elegant white carpet. The artwork surprised her. Passionate reds dominated the walls. *Must be an interior decorator.* "I'd like to have a look around Jordan's room, if that's okay?"

"Sure," he answered, starting down the hall. "It's this

way. I'm going to catch a quick shower and change. I smell like a dumpster."

She grinned. "I swear I didn't notice."

He felt himself smiling back at her as he opened a door. "I had the maid leave the room alone in case the police might have to see it."

Maggie knew at once it was Jordan's room. Posters covered the walls. The bed was unmade. Clothes were thrown everywhere. "I won't touch anything."

"What do you think you can find in this mess?"

"Maybe a friend's name. Or something that will give us an idea where she might be staying. She might be on the street or in a shelter. But it's more likely that she's with a friend. Jordan isn't like most of the kids I deal with. She's bound to have some resources."

He was impatient with that idea. "I've talked with her friends."

"Boyfriends, too?"

"She's barely thirteen! She doesn't have boyfriends."

"And you think she's not interested in boys? Take a look around this room."

Adam glanced at the posters of boy singers and male models. The flat surfaces of the room were cluttered with romance novels. He'd been in Jordan's room a thousand times, but he never noticed that his niece wasn't a young girl any more until that moment. Maybe his first instinct was right. Maybe he shouldn't have custody of Jordan. What did he know about raising a child anyway? He felt ridiculous. "I'm going to get dressed."

"I'll be in here." Maggie had never been a parent. But she knew from counseling many families that it wasn't unusual for adults not to realize that the children they cared for were interested in the opposite sex.

Her Aunt Leila was horrified when she caught Maggie sneaking in from a date when she was fourteen. They'd talked for hours about all the things that could happen to nice girls who sneak out at night. After that, their relationship was different. That's when Maggie started asking questions about her father. She learned right away that there were no answers.

She looked through the magazines that littered the floor and checked out Jordan's CD collection. There was a small diary under her Power Puff Girl bedspread. It held a list of names and phone numbers along with some doodling. The name *Scott* appeared quite a few times in flowery script. She tucked the book into her pocket.

Her search was so intense that she didn't see the lamp cord stretched from across the wall until she tripped over it. The multi-colored lamp came crashing down on the floor beside her. She sat down hard on some schoolbooks and stuffed animals.

"Are you all right?" Adam asked from the doorway.

Maggie looked up to assure him that she was fine. Her mouth stayed open in an expressive 'O' when she saw he'd left the shower wrapped only in a towel. His hair was wet and slicked back from his face. His darkly furred chest was dripping water and soap. She swallowed hard and managed to guide her eyes past his covered midsection down his legs to his feet.

"You have very big feet." She regretted her thoughtless words only a second after she said them. *You have very big feet. That was smooth.*

He glanced down at his feet. "It's a family thing. Can I help you up?" He held out his hand to her.

She stared at his hand for an instant. A thousand thoughts swirled in her brain. She could get up by herself. She wasn't hurt. It was just a polite gesture on his part. He probably didn't think anything of it at all.

But she realized when she hesitated how much she wanted to touch him. It scared her. And it *excited* her. She didn't care about all of the reasons she shouldn't feel that way.

His hand closed around hers. It was warm and wet and strong. He brought her to her feet easily. She was so close to him. She could smell the soap on his skin and see the drops of water making their way down his neck to his shoulders and chest.

"Thanks," she managed in a husky voice.

"Are you hurt?" He looked her over carefully, starting at her silky hair and ending at her scuffed boots. He could smell her perfume and see the faint freckles that dusted her cheeks. He didn't let go of her hand. It felt right in his.

"No. I'm just a little—" He quirked one brow at her, waiting for her response. Her heart flipped over in her chest. "—thirsty. I need a drink of water." She couldn't move her gaze from one drop of water that was slowly coursing down his neck. What would he do if she suddenly put her mouth to that spot to quench her thirst? *Get a grip!*

"There's water in the kitchen. Do you need to sit down?"

"No." She smiled as she scooted past him. "No. I can get it. Water's easy. Anybody can do water, right?"

Adam released her hand reluctantly. He wondered if he'd ever met anyone stranger, or more interesting, than Maggie. He watched her run down the hall towards the kitchen. She didn't look any older than Jordan. *That was it.* He went back to finish his shower. *I'm overwrought about Jordan.*

It didn't explain about what happened between them at the office. There had been that moment when they were arguing and suddenly the tension was unbearable. Something flared between them that had nothing to do with why she was there. He refused to think about that.

"What's your problem?" Maggie asked herself out loud. She looked at the water overflowing the glass she held in the sink. Had it been that long since she'd seen a man in a towel, fresh from the shower? Was she just obsessing over what Delta said about him? If so, she might as well stomp on that fire. He hadn't shown any sign of finding her interesting or attractive. Except for letting her walk down the hall without telling her that she'd passed the apartment door. *I was watching you.*

She drank two glasses of water for good measure then opened up Jordan's address book and picked up the phone. "Hi. I'm calling from The Diamond Box at Starlight Mall.

I'm trying to get in touch with Jordan Fuentes about a sweetheart bracelet she's won in a contest. Have you talked to her?"

She called three different numbers and got no answer. She left messages to call her back. She was running out of names in the little book.

"Anything?"

Maggie jumped at the sound of his voice. She put down the phone. "Not yet."

"Sorry," he said, seeing her startled move. "What are you doing?"

"Calling Jordan's friends. The chances are, someone knows where she is. Kids talk to each other. Especially when they can't or won't talk to their parents. Or in this case, her uncle."

"My niece ran away from home. I suppose I deserve that."

"Most kids don't talk to their parents. It's nothing personal." She looked up at him thoughtfully.

He sat down opposite her at the table. His dark face was clean-shaven. He'd traded one expensive suit for another. She was amazed. They were both charcoal gray. His shirt was a nice shade of blue this time. He left off his usual tie, leaving the small opening at his throat exposed.

Hastily, she made herself look back at the book in front of her. The names and numbers swam but she kept staring at them. Obviously she was having some kind of mental breakdown. Or maybe it was due to not having a date in so long. When she sorted out all of this with Jordan, she was going to call that exterminator. She needed to go out more.

"Let me take a look." He moved around behind her to look over her shoulder. "I might recognize some of the names."

Maggie felt his breath against the side of her neck as he looked at the book. She shivered and slid her chair away from him.

"Do I still smell like the dumpster?"

"No." She laughed lightly. "No. You smell very nice. Clean . . . and a little spicy."

Adam smiled into her wide blue eyes. "Are you always so honest?"

"You know the answer to that," she replied quietly. "I lied last night. Bold faced, as my aunt used to say."

"I guess I meant in your personal relationships." He reached out and slowly smoothed his hand down the side of her hair. "You have a pink feather from that stuffed parrot Jordan keeps in there."

"Oh." She made a squeaking sound in the back of her throat as she tilted her head to allow him better access. She stared at his beautifully shaped lips. "Thanks."

Chapter Four

The feather was stubborn. Adam moved closer, using his fingers to filter through the fine strands of hair. "What does your boyfriend think about you walking the streets at midnight looking for lost souls?"

"I don't have a boyfriend," she answered slowly, entranced by the feeling of his hand in her hair. "If I did, I suppose he'd have to understand."

"It hasn't been my experience that men and women in a relationship understand each other very well." He held the feather up close to her face. "There you are."

Maggie blew the tiny feather from his hand. "Then you haven't ever had much of a relationship."

He refused to look away from her slightly parted lips. "Maggie, I—"

Impulsively, she moved the short distance between them and pressed her lips quickly to his. When his mouth didn't cooperate, her eyes flew open. "I'm sorry. I guess I was carried away by the moment. I'm too emotional. I mean, Delta says I get too emotionally caught up in what I'm doing. It wasn't anything personal. I just, uh—"

Adam didn't speak. He cut off her last words of apology with his lips. He'd wanted this since that last encounter in his office. One of his hands slid behind her neck. The other drew her to her feet. The feeling of her pressed against him, hip to hip, chest to chest, made him pull her closer. His mouth touched hers lightly, like a question. Then pressed slowly, closer and deeper.

Maggie wasn't prepared for the quicksilver spread of heat and emotion that swept through her. She leaned into his solid frame and answered his mouth eagerly. Nothing else mattered at that moment but being close to him. She could feel his heartbeat through the texture of his shirt. *This can't be happening. This can't be happening. Mmmm, this is really happening!*

The phone rang, startling them both but not pushing them apart. Adam's arms still held her close to him. Maggie's fingers were still stroking the thick, damp hair at the nape of his neck. They stared at each other without speaking then slowly, moved apart. Both of them reached for the phone at the same time, knocking it to the floor.

"Hello? Hello?" a disembodied voice called out from the phone.

"Hello." Adam got to the phone first.

Maggie turned away but she smiled when she heard his voice. He sounded husky and shaken. The way any woman would want a man to sound when she'd kissed him. Maybe she hadn't done it in a while but she hadn't lost it either. She wasn't sure what just happened between them. She couldn't believe that she suddenly found him so attractive. He'd been The Ogre for so long, it was hard to think of him as anything else. But he sure didn't kiss like any ogre she'd ever read about!

"That was one of Jordan's friends," he told her, hanging up the phone.

She swung back to face him. "Oh. Has she seen Jordan?"

"Yes. At the mall." He put the phone back up on the table and fidgeted uncomfortably. What was he supposed to say now? He couldn't believe that he kissed her. Not that she seemed to mind. In fact, she kissed him back.

"Adam." Someone had to say something.

"Maggie?"

"Delta tells me that I get too emotionally worked up

about cases. I know you're vulnerable. I didn't mean to take advantage of you."

Take advantage? "Take advantage of me? I'm not some naïve boy who can't think straight because a gorgeous woman is sitting next to him!"

"Gorgeous?" Her heart did a little pirouette.

"I suppose that's why I noticed your short skirts in the first place."

"I thought you were just annoyed." She smiled a little.

"I thought so, too," he agreed reluctantly.

Maggie shook her head and wiped the smile from her face. *This is serious!* "It's just an emotional time. That's the only reason that something like this happened between us. We're not really attracted to each other. It was just a kiss of—of sympathy and feeling bad for the other person."

"Just a kiss." He searched her pretty face with his eyes. Maybe she was right. He'd never thought of her that way before. *Except for that afternoon at his office.*

Maggie hid her shaky hands in her pockets. "I suggest we put it behind us and go to the mall to try to find Jordan."

"All right." He wasn't sure whether to feel relieved or disappointed. (He was relieved, of course.) After Vickie shredded his heart, he didn't want another relationship. This attraction to Maggie was a momentary thing. She might even be right. Maybe it was an emotional response because they were looking for Jordan. He was more than willing to let her be right about it.

"Okay." *Why is he still looking at me that way? And why do I want to kiss him again?* Maggie stalked away from him, pushing the thoughts from her mind.

Adam picked up her jacket and held it out to her. "You dropped this."

"Thanks." She snatched it from him. Careful not to touch him. "Let's go."

They rode down in the elevator in total silence.

When they reached the parking lot, Adam took out his keys. "I hope that didn't make you . . . uncomfortable with me."

Maggie laughed. "*That?* Not at all."

"Happens all the time, I suppose?"

"No! I mean, I don't get *that* emotional normally but it does happen," she rattled on. "Last month it was the exterminator."

Adam was surprised. "You helped the exterminator look for his child?"

"No, I mean, I felt very emotional about the, uh, exterminator."

He opened up the passenger side door to the Mercedes. "It must be an interesting job."

"It has its moments." She started to get into the Mercedes then had a change of heart as he opened the door for himself. "You know, I think I'll take my car over to the mall."

"Maggie—"

"It's nothing to do with *that,*" she defended, moving away from the car. "I just thought that I could leave from there if we find her."

"You don't have to worry about being alone with me."

"Not at all! I was just thinking that it might be better to have both cars, you know? I'll meet you there."

She ran to her Toyota, got inside and gripped the steering wheel tightly. It didn't bother her that she kissed him. She tried to start the car. It was a very nice kiss. It was just that she shouldn't have been kissing The Ogre. She was here to help him find his niece, not seduce him!

Adam knocked on her window several times before she realized that he was there. She realized at the same time that the battery was dead and that her car wasn't going to start. She rolled down the window and looked at him.

"I think you'll have to come with me if you're going," he said, summing up the situation.

"I could take the bus," she said with a faint laugh.

"I'm sorry, Maggie. It won't happen again."

"You don't have anything to be sorry for. It was *me*. I kissed *you*!"

"Oh, *that*." He waved away her refusal. "We won't let it happen again. Does that make you feel any better?"

She considered it. "I just don't want to muddy the water between us. We have a certain . . . relationship. I don't want that to be any different after this is all over."

Adam laughed as he opened her car door. "You mean our relationship where you come to my office and ask me for money and I give you a hard time?"

"But I leave with a check anyway. That's the one. I irritate you and you infuriate me."

"No problem. We'll be exactly the same as soon as we find Jordan."

She grabbed her purse and took a deep breath. "Great. Let's go!"

The Starlight Mall was crowded even though it was a weekday. People from nearby offices were eating lunch and discussing stock portfolios. Teenagers were openly flaunting themselves since it was a half-day of school. No lurking at the sides, hoping not to be spotted by truancy officers. The high glass ceiling sparkled under the clear blue sky and colorful banners waved in the ventilation. The aroma of cinnamon rolls and coffee was everywhere.

"Where do we start?" Adam asked her as they walked into the upper story of the mall.

"We start by not announcing ourselves." Maggie realized that having Adam with her was going to make it more difficult. So many of Jordan's friends would know him. She had to find a way to play him down. She had to talk to Jordan before the girl could run away again. Usually, she wasn't looking for a runaway with the parents. If she'd been thinking, she'd have insisted that he stay at his apartment until he heard from her.

But then, if she'd been thinking, she wouldn't have kissed him. Or had her tongue hanging out when she saw him in his bath towel. Apparently, common sense wasn't going to be her strength for that day. At least not around Adam.

"How do we find Jordan by hiding? Shouldn't we be out talking to her friends?"

"No. We sort of lurk in the corners of the mall until we see someone you recognize or we see Jordan. We don't want to spook her. If we lose her here, it could take a while to track her down again."

"What do we do if we see her?" Adam watched the throngs of teenagers who all seemed to be dressed just like his niece.

"We talk to her."

"Is that it?"

"Surely you must realize if she ran away once she can do it again," Maggie demanded. "If you try to force her to go home with you, she'll be gone again tomorrow. You can't lock her in your condo and make her stay."

"Jordan has computer camp this weekend. If she isn't there, she'll lose her spot."

"Forget computer camp. You'll have to worry about that later. If we don't get her to agree to go home, she'll lose more than her spot at camp."

Adam understood what she was saying. "I just don't want her to get totally messed up by this."

"If the police pick Jordan up, what do you think will happen?"

"All right," he agreed, thinking of last night's fiasco. "We'll do it your way this time."

Maggie grinned. "I like it best that way."

"Why doesn't that surprise me?"

They spent two hours at the mall. Part of the time they walked around the outer contours of the structure, trying to blend in with store windows and shoppers. The rest of the time they stood and watched, listening to groups of teenagers as they passed them.

Adam didn't recognize any of Jordan's friends. Once, he thought he saw Jordan when they were near the food hub. But the girl turned her head and it wasn't his niece. Grim and impatient, he leaned back against the cement wall and closed his eyes. She could be out under a bridge or hitchhiking to California with the boyfriend he didn't know existed. Doubts and fears plagued him.

Maggie could see it was time for a break. "Let's eat lunch."

He opened his eyes. "Won't that be too conspicuous?"

"I think we can manage it. We can go to a restaurant that has big windows and watch the traffic go by. Maybe we'll pick her up that way."

"Okay," he said. "What sounds good? Since you fed me breakfast, I think I should buy you lunch."

"Really?"

"Yes. Why?"

She shrugged. "I don't know. I'm surprised, I guess. I thought you were too—"

"Ogrely?"

"Is that a word?"

He laughed. "You're changing the subject."

"Well, your office is so, so—"

"Quaint?"

"Old," she finished. "And you drive that old car."

"A classic with less than twenty thousand miles on it. *And* it has sentimental value. It belonged to my Uncle."

"Oh. I thought you were just cheap."

"What about the condo? Does that strike you as cheap?"

"Well, I thought you probably got that because of Jordan," Maggie teased. "You had to have somewhere to live with her. You couldn't *both* sleep in your office."

"You thought that just because I don't like to give the shelter money, I was tight with everyone else. Is that it?"

"Well, yes," she admitted. "Only a miser could resist my big eyes and short skirts."

Adam couldn't keep himself from smiling. "I thought we were going to forget I said that."

"*You* might forget, but I have a memory like an elephant."

The mall was sponsoring a 'Taste of Nations' celebration that week. It included food from various restaurants in the area that represented different cultures. Since Adam let Maggie decide where they were going to eat, she picked the festival. Lured by a periwinkle colored tent, they were seated on cushions inside with a small table between them.

"I don't know how this is going to help find Jordan," Adam complained as he tried to find a comfortable way to sit on the floor.

"It probably won't." Maggie grinned. "But it's a great way to eat Greek food for lunch."

They were served by a sloe-eyed college student who told them he was from Athens. He only had eyes for Maggie, going out of his way to adjust her cushions and bring her tea first.

"It smells lovely," she told him as he poured.

"It is called Nectar of the Gods," he responded. "Fit for a goddess like yourself."

"Are we going to eat soon?" Adam asked, already tired of the waiter trying to monopolize her time. He didn't bother trying to rationalize why he cared that the waiter was paying too much attention to her. He was learning that there was no rational explanation for things when he was with Maggie.

"Your food will be ready shortly."

"Isn't this nice?" she asked when they were alone again.

"Great."

Maggie didn't remark on his lack of enthusiasm and dug into her spanakopita when it arrived. Adam looked uncertainly at his mousaka. "What's wrong?" she asked him when she saw that he wasn't eating.

"I don't think I'm really hungry."

"That's crazy. You have to eat. Try some of mine." She held up her fork with a bite of the spinach and feta pie on it.

He looked into her eyes, swallowed hard and let her put the food in his mouth. The flaky crust melted on his tongue. "That's pretty good."

"See?" She munched away happily.

"Now you have to try some of mine," he replied, taking a spoonful to feed her.

Maggie looked at the spoon he held and shook her head. "Oh no. I'm sure this is all I can eat."

"What's wrong? Scared I'll miss your mouth and hit you in the eye?"

"No." She laughed a little at his words but it came out sounding forced. "I, uh, I'm just very full suddenly, you know?" She took a hasty sip of water to quell her sudden nervousness.

"Come on," he coaxed. "I trusted you. And you were using a fork!"

Knowing she was making too big a deal out of it, she finally agreed to try it. She closed her eyes and opened her mouth slightly as he fed her. She shivered and looked at him. He was staring intently at her lips.

"How was it?" he asked in a husky voice.

"Good," she mumbled around the onions and cheese in her mouth. "Very good."

He sighed and sat back against his cushion. The waiter fluttered around Maggie again, bringing baklava for them to sample. Adam wished he felt like his business suit was making him uncomfortable but he knew it was more. Maggie made him uncomfortable. He should've seen it from the beginning when she first came to his office. He wasn't interested in her shelter, but he was interested in *her*.

Maggie tasted the honey sweet baklava while Adam had a strong cup of coffee instead. She didn't try to tempt him with the confection. She'd learned her lesson. She didn't know what it was about him that made her suddenly so self conscious. Even though she'd agreed to forget about the kiss they'd shared at his condo, she knew it was lingering between them with every word and glance.

They could've gone through more of the tiny restaurants but Maggie suggested they go back out into the mall. "Thanks for lunch. It was good."

Adam opened the tent flap to go, content in the knowledge that she was leaving with him instead of the waiter. "I'm glad you liked it. Maggie, I—"

"It's gotten a lot more crowded," she cut him off, seeing

the intent look in his eyes. "We should really look for Jordan now."

Adam didn't say anything else. If there *was* something growing between them, there'd be plenty of time to discuss it after they found Jordan. "Where do we start?"

"Like before. We skulk around until—"

"There she is!" He pointed towards a small group of teenagers who were standing beside the pretzel stand. "We have to talk to her!"

"Wait!" Maggie tried to stop him but he was already closing in on the girl. So much for approaching her quietly.

A hot pretzel cart cut him off. Maggie sprinted forward and reached the girl before her uncle. "Jordan? Jordan Fuentes?"

The boy who stood beside Jordan flicked back his long blond hair and draped a possessive arm across her shoulders. "Who wants to know?"

This has to be Scott. "Jordan. It's me, Maggie! Maggie Madison! I'm a friend of your uncle's. Don't you remember?"

Jordan looked at her critically. "I don't think I do."

Maggie swung by the girl, knocking Scott's arm away. She tucked Jordan close to her side as she continued walking away from the group. "Jordan, think fast. Your uncle is here. He can embarrass you in front of your friends, or we can walk away like we're talking and you can tell them it's okay. When he sees us together, he won't come any closer."

"Are you serious?"

"Look past the pretzel man." Maggie gestured with her head.

Jordan looked around and saw her uncle. She looked away quickly. "Who are you *really*? Are you a private detective? Because if Uncle Adam wants to—"

"We don't have time for this. Scott is right behind us."

Jordan saw her uncle come to a stop. He didn't come any closer. Scott was reaching for her with his mouth open, about to demand to know what was going on. "I'm gonna walk for a while with—?"

"Maggie."

"Maggie." Jordan smiled at her boyfriend. "It's okay. We just have some catching up to do. I'll meet you at Smokey Joes, okay?"

Scott stopped walking. "Sure?"

"I'll be fine."

"Okay."

"What now?" Jordan whispered to Maggie who was still walking close to her side. "I don't really know you, do I?"

"No. But I'm not a private detective. My name really is Maggie Madison and I run a shelter for kids. I helped your uncle find you."

Jordan's pretty face became a mutinous mask. "I left home so I wouldn't have to see him."

"I don't blame you," Maggie quipped then righted herself. "I mean, I don't blame you for leaving home, Jordan. Sometimes you have to get away to think about things. But you have some issues you need to work out with your uncle or you'll be running forever. That's the way it works."

"I have Scott and Sally. They're helping me. I'm just fine on my own."

"But you can't go to school like that!" Maggie debated. "School officials tend to notice when you've moved away from home and you're living with your friends. That means you've screwed up your future. The one sure way to get away from your uncle is to grow up and get out on your own, totally independent of him."

"You said you were here *helping* my uncle?" Jordan smiled at her. "Does he know you're saying this to me?"

Maggie grinned. "Helping him *find* you. You're found now. What you do next is up to you. I just wanted to save you a scene with your friends. I think we can both imagine what your uncle was going to do."

"That was pretty cool," Jordan said. "I wish my uncle was that cool."

"Parents are never cool."

"He's not my father. Both of my parents are dead. He can't take their place." Jordan glanced over her shoulder to see if Adam was following them. "I mean, I know he loves me but he's always so worried about his work. You wouldn't believe how much he's at the office."

Maggie glanced back, too. Adam was standing at the rail that overlooked the escalator. She couldn't believe he was giving her that space with Jordan. He *was* desperate! "I know about your parents. But your uncle is your family now. If you have problems, you have to work it out. Just like you would if your mom and dad were still alive."

"Uncle Adam is impossible. He hates the way I dress. He hates my friends. He thinks I'm still a baby."

Maggie smiled at the rant she'd heard from a hundred other teenagers. "Yeah, I understand."

Jordan stopped walking. "You know my uncle pretty well, huh?"

"I've known him about a year now. I can see where he'd be strict."

They both looked back at him. Adam stayed where he was by gripping the handrail until his knuckles were white.

He was willing to admit that he wasn't the world's greatest surrogate parent. He was trying to do what was best for Jordan. He didn't think that included her running around after midnight with her friends. He didn't know what else to do except enforce the rules he'd set for her.

She certainly seemed to bond with Maggie right away. Maybe she needed that female support that he couldn't give her. Even so, it irritated him. He had to strain for every inch of relationship that Jordan allowed him.

"He's not a bad guy though, you know?" Jordan snapped her bubble gum. "I think he means well. He just doesn't have a clue."

"I can see that about him," Maggie agreed.

Jordan turned to her. "What about you?"

"Me?"

"Are you a parent? I bet you'd make a great mom."

"I don't think so," Maggie replied. "I take care of a lot of kids everyday but I don't have any of my own."

"Are you and my uncle . . . together?"

"No!" Maggie denied emphatically. "We don't know each other that way. We barely know each other at all. I've been to his office. He asked for my help finding you."

"I get the picture. You don't exactly like my uncle, do you?"

"He's okay. We don't always see things the same way but—"

Jordan held up her hand. "It's okay. I get it. He paid you to help him find me."

"No." Maggie rushed to reassure her. "He didn't pay me. This is what I do. I help kids get off the streets."

"I haven't exactly been on the streets," Jordan confided. "I've been staying with Sally."

"What about Sally's parents? Didn't they think that was strange?"

"They thought my uncle was out of town."

"I'm glad you weren't on the streets. It's not a nice place out there. You'll have to come by the shelter sometime. Talk to the kids. You'll see what I mean. Right now," Maggie glanced at Adam again, "I think we should talk to your uncle, don't you? Before he jumps over that rail?"

Jordan giggled. "I suppose you're right. But I'm not going home with him until we get some things straight. I'm thirteen now. He can't keep treating me like I'm a baby."

"You're right. You need to talk to him. I think you and your uncle need some counseling."

Maggie and Jordan walked back towards Adam. Jordan's friends were gone. The moment of devastation had evaporated.

"Uncle Adam." Jordan didn't look up at him.

"Jordan."

That was it. The words fizzled out between them. They were left standing in the mall not looking at each other.

Maggie had seen reunions that went from acting like the

other person wasn't there to weepy, emotional ones. This was about average.

Adam glanced at his watch. "I really need to get back to work and Jordan should be getting ready for computer camp."

Jordan's mouth tightened.

"I think it might be better to sit down together and work this out," Maggie told him.

"What's there to work out?" he argued stubbornly. "She needs to come home."

"I'm not coming home with you." Jordan's tone was defiant.

"You *are* coming home with me or I'll—"

Maggie stepped between them and laced her arms through theirs. "We're going to sit down and discuss this like civilized people. No demands and no threats. Okay?"

Jordan was sulky. "He doesn't know how."

Adam glared at Maggie. "What did you say to her?"

Maggie ignored his hostility and the fact that he was as hard and unyielding as a stick of wood beside her. It was to be expected at a time like this. "I said she should tell you how she felt and that you both need counseling. These problems are things you'll have to work out together."

He struggled to get his arm away from her but she held on tight. "What are you doing?"

She smiled at him sweetly. "Helping you handle your life."

"I don't need your help."

She inclined her head towards him and whispered, "Would you rather have this discussion with the police next month when they pick Jordan up for shoplifting food while she's out on the street? It could happen."

Adam took a deep breath. "All right."

Maggie patted his arm. "You can handle it. Just breathe. It works for me."

Adam didn't know what they were saying with their heads bent close together but he was sure it wasn't something he wanted to hear. He'd let himself in for trouble asking for Maggie's help.

Jordan glanced at him from around Maggie's shoulder. "I won't go home with him until we talk."

"What's there to talk about?" he demanded, butting into their conversation.

"That's why I left! We can't talk about anything but school and things you want me to do! I don't care what college I'm going to go to in six years. I'm young, Uncle Adam. I want to live now."

"What's that supposed to mean?"

"That's what counseling is all about," Maggie told them both. "It's good to talk about everything that's bothering you."

"I might as well move into Maggie's shelter for kids who don't have homes," Jordan told him angrily. "You can make me go home but you can't keep me there."

"What?" Maggie was stunned.

"You can't live in a homeless children's shelter," Adam replied furiously. "You're my niece and you belong at home!"

"You'll know where I am and we can talk about stuff. You can come and see me."

"You're not staying at the shelter." Adam was furious. "You don't know what goes on there!"

Maggie jumped. "Wait a minute! What are we talking about? We can't—"

"Fine." Jordan agreed. "This way, Maggie will be there to help us."

"I think we have a problem." Maggie took a deep breath and looked at the pair. They were so alike in their attitudes and features from their stubborn anger to their black hair and unusual eyes. No wonder they butted heads.

Jordan turned her golden brown eyes on Maggie. "Is that okay? Can you work that out?"

Maggie wasn't so sure. "I don't know, Jordan. We hardly have enough room for the kids we take in every night. I don't know where I'd put you."

"Please! This is important. You said yourself that we have to work out our problems."

Maggie sighed. She was going to have to learn to say no at some time in her life. Unfortunately, it wasn't at this moment. "I suppose we could put a cot in one of the rooms."

"Thanks, Maggie!" Jordan hugged her quickly. "I know this will be good for us!"

Adam looked away. It had been a long time since Jordan had impulsively hugged him. He missed the closeness they'd shared before her parents' death. He wasn't sure there was any way to get it back again. Maggie was a stranger but Jordan acted like she'd rather be with her.

Maggie saw the sadness in Adam's eyes before he could hide it. He loved his niece. "You're welcome, I think. It won't be easy. It's crowded and the plumbing is always messed up."

Jordan didn't care. "I'll be fine. It's just what I need. Thanks so much!"

But Maggie continued trying to discourage her. "There won't be much privacy and I don't know exactly where you'll sleep."

"You're not backing down, are you?" Jordan's voice shook with emotion.

"No! No, of course not. It's just that I—"

"Just breathe, Maggie," Adam consoled her sarcastically. "It works for me."

She did a quick mental calculation. She could put Jordan in her office. The girl wasn't *technically* homeless. She could even say she was a friend of a friend. The state wouldn't care where she slept. It might work. It would give them a chance to talk without the outside pressures of their normal lives. She wasn't sure how Adam would react or how long she was prepared to supervise their recovery. But she'd deal with that when the time came.

Chapter Five

They drove back to the condo in uncomfortable silence. Adam was angry that Maggie agreed to let Jordan stay at the shelter. It was just aggravating the situation, not helping. He was trapped into going along with it but he wasn't happy about it.

When he held the car door open for Maggie to get out, she brushed against him. He took a quick breath. There was something electrifying about touching her. He slammed the door in annoyance at himself and at her. Making frequent trips to the shelter to see Jordan wasn't going to help *that* situation either.

Adam and Jordan were going upstairs to pick up some clothes and other necessary items. Maggie offered to stay with Jordan but the girl turned her down. She was surprised that Jordan went with Adam so willingly. She obviously wasn't afraid that he'd go back on his word.

"Once he makes a deal, he doesn't go back on it," Jordan explained. "I guess that's why he's so good at his job. Too good, if you ask me."

"You said that before about him working all the time," Maggie told her. "Have you thought that maybe you need some extra attention from him? Maybe both of you would like to be closer."

"I'm not a kid!" Jordan stomped off to the elevator.

"All right. I'll see you later then." Maggie shrugged off

Jordan's temper tantrum. She turned to leave but Adam wasn't finished yet.

He waited until his niece was in the elevator to confront Maggie. "This isn't necessary. She doesn't have to live with you at the shelter. I'll deal with Jordan."

She glared at him. "You know, Jordan just told me that you never back out on a deal. I think she admires that about you. Don't blow it."

"You know, you'll have to see more of me," he warned as she walked past him.

"I can handle it if you can." She smiled at him. "I'll see you at the shelter."

Maggie's little Toyota started right up. It was obviously part of the conspiracy to ruin her life. When she reached the shelter, she hurried through to her office. It was a mess, of course. Papers and checks were lying around everywhere. There were cases of donated canned goods and last year's blow up kiddie pool. She started shoving some of the stuff into a closet.

"Where have you been?" Delta wondered, finding her there. "And what are you doing?"

"Trying to push this into the corner." Maggie panted as she strained against the old wood desk. "You could help."

"Have you lost your mind?"

"The Ogre's niece is moving in with us until they can settle a few of their differences," Maggie answered.

"You must be crazy!" Delta didn't move to help her.

"I'm going to charge him room and board while she's here." Maggie collapsed on top of the desk.

Delta moved right up next to her and leaned her weight against the desk. "Why didn't you say so, girl? Let's get this furniture moved. I can see a whole new future for us in this business. Instead of poor children whose parents leave them behind because they don't have enough money to support them, we could set up a shelter for rich kids whose parents could pay plenty to keep them here."

"Delta—"

"What? A girl can dream, can't she?"

They pushed the desk into the corner and started to move boxes of shelter records and a few broken chair parts. "Speaking of dreams, how's Dan?"

Delta smiled wickedly. "He's good, you know? *Real* good!"

"I take it you mean that in a bad way?"

"You got that right. He's always so nice. Who would've thought that under that sweet exterior was a molten interior."

Maggie put her hands over her ears. "Too much information!"

"You're jealous."

"I am not!"

Delta studied her friend. "You've got a glow about you. And I don't believe it's that halo everyone always wants to give you! Did you put in a call to the exterminator?"

"No." Maggie stacked some boxes on a chair then pushed it all into the closet. She leaned against the door to close it.

"It's not *him*, is it?" Delta put her hands over her mouth and her eyes rolled up towards the ceiling. "It's not The Ogre, is it? Is he hot for you like I said?"

"Don't be silly!"

"It's him, isn't it?" Delta stopped moving boxes of canned pineapple.

"It's not him. There's nothing between us. He doesn't even like Greek food!"

"Maggie?"

"Never mind!"

"*Maggie!*"

"Delta, I don't want to talk about The Ogre!" Maggie swung around. Jordan and Adam were standing in the doorway.

Adam's face was dark with anger.

Maggie shook her head. She just couldn't win with this man.

Jordan was grinning broadly. "Who's The Ogre?"

"Never mind." Adam and Maggie barked at the same time.

"Welcome, Mr. Fuentes!" Delta took his hand then turned to the girl who'd come with him. "You must be Jordan. I'm Delta Sommers, Maggie's partner. Let me show you around the house."

Jordan looked at her uncle. Adam nodded. "Go ahead. I have a few things I'd like to say to Maggie before you move in."

Maggie moved another box into a corner and dusted off her hands. She wasn't in any hurry to be alone with him. "We might as well go with them. You should know your way around the place too."

"In a minute, please." Adam's polite tone was glacial.

Delta laughed and urged Jordan out of the door. "Come on, Sweet Pea. I'm sure we don't want to be in the middle of this ruckus."

"Was she calling Uncle Adam an ogre?" Jordan's voice trailed innocently out the door behind Delta. "Cool!"

When they were alone, Adam confronted Maggie. "Well?"

"Well . . . what?" She kept moving boxes around the room.

"Since this was *your* idea, would you mind not calling me that name while Jordan's here?"

Maggie took a deep breath. "Fine. But I wasn't calling you that name. Only *referring* to you."

"Maybe you could stop using it at all while she's here, if that isn't too much to ask?"

"I'm sorry." She knew that she was wrong to call him names. Especially when he might be around to hear them. She'd have to watch it. "I won't use it again while you're here."

Adam wasn't satisfied. "We both know why you did this. You wanted to get even with me. I think it's kind of low to use Jordan."

Maggie couldn't believe it. Of all the ungrateful, miserable people she'd ever met, he was the worst. "I did this to help you and your niece. I don't have any ulterior motives. I'm happy feuding with you over donations for the shelter the way we always have."

He didn't believe her. "And you don't feel even the smallest bit of remorse that you encouraged her to stay here?"

"If you wouldn't have been so smug about all of it, we wouldn't be having this conversation." Maggie caught her runaway tongue but it was too late.

"So you admit it!"

She bounced down another box of pineapple. "Okay. I'm sorry that I got between you and Jordan. I didn't mean that to happen. I was really trying to help. But you were trying to make *me* the fall guy for her not staying here. That wasn't fair!"

Adam tried to pace the room. His long legs were confined to an angry shuffle by all of the boxes. "She's my niece!"

"That doesn't give you the right to take it out on me. The two of you have problems. You're her guardian. Act like you care."

"That's what I was trying to do. Until you came up with this ridiculous idea."

"You weren't doing a very good job of it!" She kicked the last box that was stubbornly refusing to move. But she regretted her moment of temper right away when pain shot through her toe. "Ouch!"

Adam saw her step back quickly. She was about to fall over another box. He put out his hands and caught her before she fell. *Idiot! You should have let her fall!*

"Th—thanks." She was perched precariously on her toes between the box she'd kicked and the one behind her. She wasn't sure she could move either way without falling. So she held on to him and smiled.

Adam was delighted by her dilemma. Maggie had maneuvered him into a difficult position with Jordan. It was only fair that she was in a difficult position right now.

But he couldn't leave her standing there like some wind-blown ballerina. He swept his arm behind her to lift her over the box. She didn't weigh anything. But she was warm and vibrantly alive in his arms. The little red dress she wore slid higher as he moved her closer to him. He tried not to notice, but Maggie was impossible to ignore.

"Uh, thanks." She held herself against him awkwardly, not sure where to put her hands. Her heart was beating too fast and she was having a hard time breathing. *It's only the Ogre. Nothing to get excited about.*

"Better?" he asked when she was on her feet again.

"Much better. Thanks."

There was only a small spot where the old wood floor was showing between the desk, the chairs and the boxes. They stood on that spot, pressed closely to each other.

Adam's right arm was still around her waist. He told himself to move away from her. But the command didn't make it from his brain to his body. "I'm sorry about trying to make you the scapegoat for getting Jordan back home."

She blinked. He totally threw her off with a single sentence. Just when she thought she had him neatly categorized. Just when she thought he was going to be exactly the way she thought he was going to be. It didn't help that he was still holding her close. She could see the tiny smile lines that ran from his eyes and his lips. And there was a hint of curl in his thick black hair. "That's okay. I was wrong to go along with it. There's not much room. She's going to be miserable here."

He picked up on her train of thought. "She won't want to stay long then, will she?"

"You have a devious mind." Maggie cleared her throat. Was that *her* voice?

"I got that way from constantly trying to outwit you. Having Jordan around only makes it worse."

Maggie wiggled a little and Adam let her go. There wasn't enough room to move away from him without trying to step across another box. She folded her arms protectively across her chest. "Well, anyway. Jordan will be staying here in the office."

"Thanks."

She moved another box out of the way. "But I will have to ask for room and board for her. Our funds won't stretch—"

Adam picked up the box that she was trying to shove with her foot. "Why am I not surprised?"

She didn't know what to say. When a path was cleared to the door, she breathed a sigh of relief. "We should really catch up with Delta and Jordan. The tour might convince you to become a regular contributor to the shelter."

"You never give up, do you?"

She grinned. "What do you think?"

They caught up with Delta easily since she'd been stopped a hundred times after she left the office.

"This is gonna be great," Jordan told Maggie when they joined them. "Thanks again."

"Don't thank me yet," Maggie said. "We have a chore roster and rules that have to be followed. We're probably stricter than your uncle is at home."

"Maybe." Jordan's gaze snaked away. "What about friends? Can I have friends visit?"

"At certain times." 'Friends' must mean Scott, Maggie thought.

"Okay." Jordan looked back over her shoulder at Adam. "If nothing else, it teaches *him* that he can't control everything I do."

That didn't sound like a winning strategy but Maggie had already agreed to let her stay. Adam was going to have to get used to the idea that his niece was rebellious. She was going to give him a hard time in the next few years. He might as well be prepared for it.

Somehow during the rest of the walk through the shelter, Delta ended up with Jordan. Maggie was next to Adam. She didn't see her do it but Maggie swore that Delta manipulated the dynamics. They needed to have a long talk about Adam. She didn't want Delta pushing him on her all the time just because *she* believed they were right for each other.

"This is a nice place," Adam started innocently enough when Maggie was walking beside him.

"Thanks. We work hard to give the kids a good place to get their lives back together."

"And the whole family you told me about at the office?" he asked as they walked through the upstairs hall.

"That was unusual," she countered. "But we couldn't turn them away. Most of the time it's the family that needs the long-term help. The kids being abandoned is just the by-product."

They went downstairs. Adam peeked in at the TV room where a dozen or so kids were congregated. "My mother and father came here from Mexico with nothing but a crying baby. They survived until they could make enough money for a house and my father started his business."

"It's the survival part that bothers me," she explained carefully. "It's what happens to people while they're trying to survive. The world is a different place, Adam. Even you must be aware of that."

"If you mean drugs and crime, I'm aware of that. My office has been broken into twice in the past year. It was never burglarized in the years my father was there."

"That's what I'm talking about. Your parents probably found other people they took shelter with. They probably didn't live on the street. But the community has changed. People aren't so willing to take in strangers anymore."

"Here's our chore roster." Delta reached the end of the short tour. "You'll be up here, too, Jordan. As soon as we decide what you're going to do."

"Will I have to go to school?"

"Of course!" her uncle told her bluntly with a glance at Maggie. He defied her to argue with him on *that* point.

"Do the other kids here go to school?" Jordan asked obliviously.

"They do." Maggie jumped in to help Adam. "If they can't go to the local school, they go to a shelter school a few miles away. Everybody needs to go to school."

"Okay."

"Good. Now we've got that over, let's see what we can do about getting you settled." Delta took Jordan along with her. Before she left, she managed to give Maggie a knowing smile. "We'll need a cot from upstairs."

"We haven't finished moving the boxes." Maggie couldn't believe that Delta was still trying to set her up with Adam. What was she thinking?

"I'm sure Adam wouldn't mind helping you with those, would you, Adam?"

"No." Adam already felt like his life was being manipulated out of his control. What was one more thing? "Of course not."

Maggie surrendered to the inevitable. Jordan might lose interest in living at the shelter after a few days. If not, Adam would be around for a while. "Fine."

He followed her back to the office. "Where do you want to start?"

Maggie ignored him. She struggled with a large crate of donations from a local store.

He watched her for a moment then lifted it away from her. "Where do you want it?"

"Uh, the hall for now, thanks."

"I don't think it will take Jordan long to get homesick for her Game Boy and her own TV, do you?"

"It's a different situation." Maggie tackled another box that she put on top of the crate in the hall. "But she might learn from it, too."

Adam added two more boxes to her stack. "I can't imagine Jordan doing chores."

"You mean you don't have certain responsibilities for her outside of her school work?"

"No. I guess I wanted to make things as easy for her as I could."

Maggie understood. "You felt sorry for her."

Adam's eyes were filled with pain when he looked at her. "I felt sorry for both of us. I couldn't believe that John and Leslie were gone. Jordan was in a state of shock for a long time. I knew I couldn't give her parents back to her. I just wanted her to be happy."

Maggie took pity on him. "You did the best you could. Nothing can prepare you for becoming a parent overnight. But Jordan isn't in a state of shock anymore. She's growing up. She needs your guidance and your acceptance. She doesn't have anyone else to turn to."

He moved a chair into the hall. "When we were her age, my brother and I worked with my father every day after school. That's how we learned to be responsible."

"Well, you didn't start with Jordan that way. You gave her a Game Boy and her own room and a cell phone. She doesn't have that sense of responsibility that carried you through to adulthood. You're going to have to allow for Jordan being young and wanting to push the limits you put on her."

Adam looked around the office. There was an open space barely big enough for a cot. Jordan wouldn't even make it past her first day. Maggie was right. He'd spoiled her. She was used to the good life. A runaway kid's shelter wasn't going to be the thrill that she expected. Or at least that was his plan. She'd be back home in a day or two. He turned to open the closet door behind him.

"No!" Maggie tried to stop him but it was too late. Everything she and Delta had pushed into the closet came tumbling down on him.

Frantically, she threw herself on the scuffed wood floor and started digging through the rubble. Broken chairs and the deflated kiddie pool had fallen last, covering Adam's face. She hoped he wasn't seriously injured. She picked up a box of office supplies and the box split open. It showered them both with pencils, notepads, and Dilbert cartoons. "Adam? Are you all right? Should I call 911?"

He pushed a jacket and part of a bicycle away from his face. "That closet is a deathtrap!"

"I know. I tried to stop you." She moved debris off of him, reaching further and further. Without realizing it, she was laying on top of him on the floor. "I'm so sorry. I didn't think anyone was going to go in there."

"I'm all right." He tried to move. A gorgeous leggy brunette was squirming around on top of him, trying to move the clutter from the closet. Her hair tickled his nose. He reached his hand down to move her away with the desk pads and bottles of glue. He encountered a warm, smooth thigh where her skirt rode up in her haste to free him. *Not that there was much of it to ride up.* Just thinking about her that way made his body go into hyper drive.

"I'm sorry. Let me help you." She worked her way down his torso. Reaching to move a pad of paper, she accidentally grabbed his leg. "Oh! Sorry."

"I think I can handle the rest." He moved her hand from his leg.

She shifted position so that she could look into his face. "I tried to warn you."

"I'm fine. If you could just move to one side or the other."

Maggie looked at her precarious position on him. "Oh, sorry!"

"Maggie—"

She pulled a yellow ducky mask from the top of his head and started laughing. "You're a very big duck!"

Her blue eyes sparkled down into his. Her smile was contagious. He laughed with her until he realized that he couldn't breathe. Part of it was his reaction to her laughter. The other part was her perfume. She smelled so sweet. Like a flower garden in the rain. It wasn't hard to tangle his hands in her hair and bring her face closer. It was even easier to kiss her soft lips.

Maggie stopped laughing when she knew he was going to kiss her again. She could've moved. She could've said something. Instead she found herself closing her eyes and taking a deep breath.

Kissing him was wonderful. It was hot fudge sundaes and walking in the warm summer rain all rolled up into one male package she couldn't resist. She forgot the exterminator. She was lying on the floor in the middle of her closet trash. She didn't care. She clung to him. She smiled in satisfaction when she heard him give a tiny little groan.

"This is stupid," he whispered, breaking the connection their lips were making. "I'm not some kid who rolls around on the floor with a girl."

"You know, I like you much better when you don't talk!" She put her mouth back on his to make sure he understood.

"Excuse me? I'm looking for Jordan Fuentes." A tall, red-haired woman stood in the doorway. "I'm Lynn Hargrove from Social Services."

Adam tried to straighten his shirt and make some kind of order out of his suit coat. His black hair was standing straight up on his head where Maggie's fingers had combed through it. One of his shoes was missing. "I'm Adam Fuentes, Jordan's uncle."

The look on Ms. Hargrove's face was like something from a comedy show. No one could look that way naturally. "You're Jordan's guardian?"

"Yes." He scrambled to his feet and helped Maggie to hers. "What can I do for you? Is Jordan in some kind of trouble?"

"I was told that Jordan would be staying here for a while. Her school is concerned about her." She glanced at Maggie. "You must be Maggie Madison. I've heard a lot about you."

Maggie knew she looked like she'd been rolling on the floor with a really delicious man and it was true. Every tasty morsel of it. She didn't know this woman and she wasn't making any excuses for her behavior to a stranger. She held out her hand. "Yes, I'm Maggie Madison."

Lynn Hargrove barely touched her cold fingertips to Maggie's. Her eyes mirrored her disapproval. "Is Jordan Fuentes staying here with you?"

Maggie glanced at Adam. "Yes."

The social worker took out a small notebook. "Has there been some trouble with the police?"

"No," Maggie answered honestly. "She's here as my guest."

Adam wasn't so at ease. "How did you know we were here?"

"When a child is absent from school with no explanation," Ms. Hargrove explained, "we begin to look for the problem. In this case, we had reason to believe Jordan left home. She appeared to be staying with friends. The school was unable to get in contact with you."

"There really isn't a problem," Maggie intervened between their dark stares. "Jordan is here because she needed a place to stay while the contractors take the asbestos out of their condo."

"Asbestos?" The social worker glanced through her notes. "No one said anything about asbestos."

"I think we should all sit down in the family room," Maggie invited. "I'm sure we can straighten this out."

Ms. Hargrove closed her notebook. "Well I assumed when I heard she was here, that Jordan was a runaway as her friend's mother assumed."

Maggie laughed. "Oh no. When I heard about the problem, I invited Jordan here to stay. She's been so much help around here."

"Really?" Ms. Hargrove dusted off the lemon yellow chair in the family room before sitting down. "I'm afraid the school just didn't understand the situation."

Adam glanced uneasily at Maggie. He was grateful for her intervention. But he had to wonder what it was going to cost him.

Jordan came in and sat beside her uncle on the pale green sofa. "This is a cool place. I'm going to like staying here."

Delta joined the group, smiling at Ms. Hargrove. "You must be Jordan's mother."

Maggie almost jumped out of the yellow chair. "No, Delta. This is Ms. Hargrove from Social Services. She's here because she thought Jordan ran away from home."

Delta introduced herself to the social worker. "Sorry. I guess I just didn't know what was going on."

Jordan nodded. "Me either."

They sat there awkwardly for a few more minutes. Maggie chattered about the shelter, offering to take Ms. Hargrove on a tour. No one else spoke. They were all afraid of saying the wrong thing.

Adam didn't say a word until the social worker walked out the door. "That was some fast talking."

Delta laughed. "So, what was going on? What did I miss?"

"Nothing much," Maggie told her. "I just didn't want Jordan's leaving home to go on her permanent record."

"I think it's time for some oatmeal cookies and iced tea," Delta replied. She glanced at Jordan. "Now's as good a time as any for you to start helping out, honey."

Jordan was happy to go with her. It was still a unique experience being there.

Maggie glanced at Adam when they were gone. "You don't have to thank me."

He smiled. "I don't know what to say."

"I have that effect on people. I'm surprised you didn't notice before."

"I noticed. You leave a trail of good deeds a mile behind you." He looked at her eager face and bright eyes. "Thanks for your help; now I need to go and get some work done."

"I'll talk to you tomorrow and we'll set up a time for counseling. You can come by and see Jordan whenever you like."

"All right." He wasn't sure about Maggie counseling them but he was willing to try anything at that point. Hopefully, Jordan would get past this problem quickly.

Maggie sighed and put her hands in her pockets as she watched him leave in his old Mercedes. She wasn't good at leaving things unsaid and she felt like the day left a whole pack of them. It had always been tough for her to leave issues unresolved. Mostly, she kept talking until there was a resolution. It annoyed some people but it worked for her. She just wasn't sure what she should say to Adam about her turbulent emotions, if anything.

"Well?" Delta wanted to know everything when Adam was gone.

Conscious of other ears that were listening, Maggie pulled her into the office and shut the door. "He kissed me."

"Go on!"

"He kissed me after the closet opened and everything fell on him. Then I sort of kissed him."

Delta began to sort through the mess that they were standing in. "So, Ms. Hargrove walked in and you two were going at it?"

"Something like that." Maggie slammed twelve bottles of glue into a shoebox. "He just kissed me."

"And you sort of kissed him. These details I can handle."

"I'm not talking to you about it."

"Maggie, you know I can pry it out of you. Don't make me use my power on you."

"Delta, I don't know why this is happening between us. But it can't be good. The first time—"

"You kissed The Ogre before? And you didn't tell me? Am I psychic or what? Where's the paper? I need to play the horses!"

"You're an idiot."

Delta got close to her and raised her black brows. "Well? How was it?"

"It was . . ." Maggie grinned and her eyes got wide, ". . . *awesome*. My hands are still shaking."

"So you plan on it happening again?"

"I don't! We don't have anything in common. Except for a need to annoy one another. That can't be good."

"And the *hots* for each other," Delta reminded her. "I know a lot of people who've based life-long commitments on less."

"Well, that's not what I'm looking for." Maggie pushed some invoices into an envelope. "Well, not *all* the time at least. Once in a while, it might be nice."

A sudden, loud gush of water was followed by screams from upstairs. Both women groaned.

"Your turn," Delta told Maggie. "While you were out with Mr. Hot Lips, I had to take care of it twice."

"We need to call a plumber."

"Why? Need a *real* man to take your mind off The Ogre? Not that he's too bad, mind you. Put him in a uniform and he'd be *ripe* for the picking!"

"I promised we wouldn't call him that again while Jordan's staying here."

"You shouldn't make those kind of promises in the heat of passion!"

Maggie left her there without another word.

Chapter Six

It was barely after six when Maggie was awakened by a clanging sound coming from the bathroom. She'd done what she could with the toilet the night before and had to make plans to call someone the next day. It was close to midnight before she took off her soaking clothes and climbed into bed.

Now she groaned as she realized that the first wave of students must've messed it up again. Then she realized that it was Sunday. No one was going to school today. She almost fell back asleep again with that realization, but the clanging started again.

Dragging herself out of bed, she pulled on her bunny robe but left off her slippers as she raced for the bathroom. She didn't want to get them wet if the toilet was going crazy again. Yawning, she grabbed the wrench she'd been hitting the ancient pipes with last night. She stopped dead as she saw Adam lying on the bathroom floor. "What are you doing here?"

"Trying to repair your water problem," he explained, without looking at her. "I did some plumbing work when I was in college. I think these pipes must've been here since before the Civil War but I'll see what I can do with them."

"Thanks," she mumbled, not sure what to make of it.

"What's going on in there?" Delta asked, meeting her in the hall.

"The O—I mean, Adam Fuentes, is fixing our pipes."

"Oh." Delta yawned and groaned. "Does he have to be so *loud* on a Sunday morning?"

"I'm not sure I'm even awake yet," Maggie answered. "I'm going to get dressed and then we'll see if he's *really* here."

The clanging from upstairs continued. Either the kids didn't hear it or were ignoring it since it was Sunday. But Maggie was now awake. She couldn't go back to sleep. She sat by the window in the kitchen with a cup of coffee in her hands and waited for the house to come to life around her.

"Is Jordan up yet?" Adam's deep voice took her by surprise.

"No, not yet." She turned to face him. His voice sent a shiver up her spine. "We let everyone sleep late on the weekend. The coffee's hot. Help yourself if you'd like a cup while you're waiting."

"Thanks." He cleared his throat. "I'm sorry if I woke you. I was just, uh, trying to be useful. To thank you for what you did for Jordan."

Maggie was surprised that he felt that way and amazed to see him out of a suit for once. Instead he was wearing black sweats that clung to him, making her look away quickly. "I thought you were angry about it."

Adam poured a cup of coffee and took a sip. "I hope I'm not a total moron. I know that you meant well with Jordan. And maybe you were right. She might have come home with me last night and been gone again this morning. I know I can't stop her. I'm not happy about the situation but maybe we can accomplish something by her being here."

"I'm glad I could help. I hope you can resolve your differences." She couldn't believe Adam was saying those things to her. Maybe he'd been hit on the head with a pipe wrench.

"Thanks. I want to help out while she's here. I'm not a professional but I'm pretty handy. I noticed a few things that need doing when I was here last night. I guess you were right. Taking the tour convinced me to take an interest."

Maggie's blue eyes narrowed. "But I still have to charge you room and board for Jordan."

He laughed at her. "You're obsessed, Maggie Madison! Always concerned about money. I'll pay the room and board. But I'd like to do these other things for you too."

"All right. Thanks." She said the polite words but she was suspicious. What was he up to?

Adam began cataloging the things he felt needed to be done. Maggie listened but kept wondering when he was going to come to the catch. When he finished the list and told her what he planned to do, she stared at him.

"Is that okay?" he asked finally when she didn't say anything.

"Sure." She collected herself. None of this made sense to her but she was getting used to feeling that way around him. "I suppose I should get ready for breakfast. The kids will start wandering down anytime now."

There was a loud thump from upstairs followed by cheering. It sent her sprinting up to find out what was wrong. Just because it was early didn't mean there couldn't be trouble.

"He started it!" Robbie, one of the older boys, accused when she walked into the room.

Kevin, the new boy, was lying on the floor with a bloody nose. "He hit me twice!"

"You were coming at me!"

"All right, that's enough!" Maggie reached down to help Kevin up from the floor. She didn't see him shake his fist at Robbie. Before she could move away, Robbie charged, his fists flying at Kevin.

Adam walked in behind Maggie just as one of Robbie's punches landed on her face. The force almost knocked her off her feet. He pulled the boys apart and sent them each to a separate side of the room. Then he looked at Maggie. "Are you okay?"

"Yeah." She moved her face experimentally then questioned the boys, "What's this all about?"

Robbie glanced at Kevin. "Nothing."

"Nothing," Kevin repeated.

Maggie wanted to shake both of them for answers. "Okay. That's it. You're both pulling extra duties today. No outside activities for the weekend. And you're both on thirty-day trial. You know what that means."

Kevin punched a pillow and Robbie kicked the side of the bed. But neither boy said anything else to her.

"You should put some ice on that." Adam studied the bruise near Maggie's eye as they left the room.

"I will."

"What's thirty-day trial?"

"When they fight or steal from each other, something serious, they have thirty days that they have to stay clean. If they repeat again in that time, they're out of the house."

"That sounds pretty strict."

"It's the only way to run the shelter. Going out after the door's been locked or using drugs is even more serious. There's no trial for that. We can get some hard cases in here. Sometimes we can help and sometimes we can't. But we have to protect all of the kids."

"It must be hard for you to give up on any of them."

"Why do you say that?"

"Because I know personally that you *never* give up!"

Maggie smiled then put a hand to her face. "Oww, that hurts."

Adam sat her down in the kitchen and wrapped some ice in a clean dishcloth. "You're going to have a shiner."

She put the ice against her eye slowly. It hurt worse but she knew it would keep the swelling down. "Thanks."

"Always putting yourself in the middle, aren't you? Between me and Jordan and those two boys. Someday you'll be Saint Maggie."

She grimaced. "I don't see myself that way. I like to help but I'm not weird or anything."

"Yeah." He pretended to consider the matter as he studied her pretty face. Her nose was so cute. And she had a wonderful mouth. The plan to help out at the shelter had been hatched in desperation at 2:00 A.M. that morning. He figured it would give him an opportunity to solve both of his new emotional crises: his relationship with Jordan and getting to know Maggie. "I didn't mean that you're weird. Just dedicated. This place is your life."

She felt the full force of his sexy eyes. Was he talking to her? Commiserating with her? *Talk about weird!* "I know what you're going to say. Any man would have to be crazy to get involved with someone like me. Delta says it all the time."

"Is that what I was going to say?"

"Weren't you?" She hid her interest in his answer by trying to take a stubborn sticker off of a new salt shaker.

"I don't think so." He took the shaker from her and ripped off the sticker before handing it back. "But he'd have to be aware of your level of involvement."

Her hand tingled from his touch. She gripped her coffee cup and the ice pack with renewed vigor. "Either way, it boils down to the same thing, doesn't it?" She caught herself staring at his lips as he drank his coffee then quickly looked away. It still made her a little breathless thinking about the kisses they'd shared. "I'm a loner anyway. It works for me."

Adam caught her gaze and felt a strong urge to take her into his arms. Just looking at her reminded him that her skin was soft and smooth. And she smelled so good. The scent was all hers. He took a deep, deep breath. "Does it? I used to feel that way about myself."

"Really? What changed your mind?" She held the ice away from her face. "How does that look?"

He leaned closer to her to look at the rapidly forming bruise on her face. It was slightly purple already. "Not swollen but you should keep it on there a few more minutes."

"So what changed your mind?" She stared directly into

his eyes and wished her heart would stop pumping so hard when she was around him.

He hadn't noticed those three sweet little freckles by the corner of her mouth or the engaging contour of her lips. Her eyes were open wide as she looked at him. The bright blue engulfed him. "Meeting someone."

"Oh?" Her heart felt a little strange, like someone had stepped on it but she persevered. "Is this someone recent? It could be good for Jordan and for you to have a woman in your lives."

Adam cleared his throat and moved away from her. "She's new. I don't know if we'll have any kind of relationship, but—"

Maggie winced as she put the ice back on her eye. "I suppose it was a surprise for you after being alone for so long."

"Yeah." He laughed. "Nothing like this has happened to me for a while."

Maggie hid behind her ice pack. "You mean you don't date?"

"I'm sure I *used* to date. I just can't remember the last time. Between the business and Jordan, I barely have enough time to sleep."

"Something like that could be helpful to Jordan," Maggie said in a very practical tone of voice. She was not saying that to give him any ideas. Just because he kissed her didn't mean anything. As his counselor, if he was interested in another woman, she should encourage him. "She'd see you going out and realize that you're not as old and lacking in fun as you seem."

"I suppose that's true." He sighed. "I don't get away from work enough. Old habits die hard."

"I have the same problem," she agreed. "I only get a couple of nights out a month and I usually fall asleep before I can go out. But you should make the effort. It would be good for you."

"You think so?" His eyes narrowed on her face. "Then maybe we could go out together."

Maggie eyed him warily but her heart started beating a little faster. "I don't know. I don't think that would be such a great idea. I mean, what about the new woman? We shared a couple of kisses, but that doesn't mean anything. You should be looking for a relationship."

He leaned close to her and smiled into her good eye. "Okay. But we could start with a date. I think I still remember how that goes."

"You mean *I'm* the new woman?" She searched for words while she tried to correct the sudden squeak in her voice. "I don't think that's such a good idea, Adam. Sometimes, when things like this happen, people *feel* close but they're really not."

"Maggie," he replied quietly, "I'm thirty-five years old. I haven't had many relationships with women. But I think I know what it feels like to be attracted to someone."

"But—"

He laughed and touched a careful kiss to her lips. "The brave Maggie Madison isn't afraid to get in the middle of a relationship with an ogre, is she?"

Maggie felt a shiver slip down her spine at the sound of his laughter. It was deep and rich. Exciting in some way that she didn't want to question. She liked it. "You should do that more often."

"What's that?"

"Laugh. You have a very nice laugh."

"Thanks. You have a very nice . . ." His gaze rushed over her pretty face and big blue eyes. Then he saw that her skirt was barely covering her thighs.

"A very nice . . . ?" she prompted.

"Smile. You have a very nice smile."

"And you think we should go out . . . together," she clarified. "You don't think we'll end up killing each other?"

"There's only one way to find out."

"Okay," she decided finally. "We could try it, I suppose. When and where?"

"We'll work that out. I can probably be free when you are."

"All right." The kids started dropping into the kitchen, looking for breakfast. "I guess I should get some food ready."

"Let me help," he offered. "What are you making?"

Adam looked through the noisy house after breakfast was over. He'd helped Maggie make and serve oatmeal to a dozen kids who crowded into the kitchen. He thought it went pretty well. Even telling her that he wanted to go out with her wasn't a complete fiasco. She didn't turn him down flat anyway.

He'd left her settling some disagreement between two girls about a pair of shoes. Jordan had breezed in and out without saying much. She was busy with her assigned chores. One of them was taking out the trash. He couldn't believe she'd want to do that for long.

There wasn't anything he wouldn't do for Jordan, including give her up if he thought it was the right thing to do. It would break his heart not to have her in his life everyday. She reminded him so much of his brother. But maybe she needed something more than he could give her.

It was difficult staying in business after his father died. John was living in Spokane at the time. A few months later, he and Leslie moved to Atlanta. Everything was all right again. He and John did everything together. Then John and Leslie went away for their ill-fated anniversary trip. Telling Jordan that her parents were dead was the hardest thing Adam had ever done.

Leslie's great aunt from Vancouver attended the funeral and offered to take Jordan back to Canada with her. She could offer the girl a good life and plenty of female companionship. But he didn't want to let go of her. Wasn't that why he pushed himself so hard to make it work between them? Maggie would probably say it was something he needed help with. He held on too fiercely to the people he loved.

But maybe it was time he learned that every family wasn't like the one he grew up in. Maybe it was time to let Jordan make up her own mind. If she'd be happier with her aunt, he'd be wrong to keep her there with him.

He wandered into the shelter office where Jordan slept. It was instinct that made him pick up the first group of bills he saw and organize them into piles. He started working for his father, organizing things around his office, when he was twelve. By the time he was sixteen, he was working full time and going to school. He worked his way through college, at his father's request. He was the first person in his family to go to college. Afterwards, he helped send his brother to school.

Before he knew it, he was deep into the inner workings of the shelter. Such as they were. It was incredible to him that Maggie and Delta were able to tell their heads from their butts with the mess their system was in.

It only took an hour to organize and categorize the bills and donations. Without looking at Maggie's computer and the rest of her books, it was impossible for him to know what they should do. He thought she might be better served with him doing the shelter's accounting than repairing their plumbing. They were definitely in need of an accountant.

He went for another cup of coffee at about eleven and found Delta sitting at the table with a cup in her hands. He almost walked back out of the room again.

She saw him first and smiled. "Come on in. Might as well make a party of it."

Two boys ran by him and out the back door. "This place is a zoo!"

"I know. It's always like this. Sometimes worse. What are you doing here?"

He explained his handyman tasks to her. "I have a lot to think about right now. It's good to do things that aren't so stressful." He took a chair across from her. "Maggie gave me plenty to consider. Is she like that with everyone?"

Delta laughed. "She's good at that! When I met that girl, I was a mess! My husband had just died and I felt like my whole world was gone. She gave me plenty to think about too."

"I'm sorry," Adam muttered, feeling awkward. "Your husband must've been very young."

"Twenty-eight. Whoever expects someone to die at twenty-eight? He had his whole life in front of him."

"What happened?" Adam sat back. "Sorry. If you'd rather not talk about it—"

"That's okay." Delta patted his hand. "Matt had leukemia. I knew it when I married him. But we had ten great years together. I wouldn't give them up for anything."

"So Maggie dragged you into the shelter to work when he died?"

"Pretty much. Next thing I knew, my life was so full, I didn't have time to turn around much less feel sorry for myself! These kids need so much. We can't even start to help them all. This house seemed so big when we first moved in but now we could use a place twice as big!"

"That's why she's always out campaigning for funds." Adam hoped she didn't think he was pumping her for information about Maggie. He was, but he hoped she didn't think he was.

"Maggie is a strange lady. You'd think she was raised on the street or something as dedicated as she is to these kids." Delta sipped her coffee. "She was abandoned by her father, you know."

He swallowed a sip of coffee. "She mentioned that to me."

"He was a musician of some kind. She won't talk about him. Her mother died when she was four. She can't even remember her much. Her father packed her up and took her to her mother's sister to raise. She said he didn't even say goodbye, but who knows? She was young and hurt. Who knows what made him leave? Maybe he didn't think he could raise a child, especially a girl, by himself."

It was an uncomfortable parallel for Adam. "He never tried to contact her? Never saw her again?"

"For all she knows, honey, he's been dead since that day! She tried to get her Aunt Leila to look for him when she was growing up but the woman didn't want to give him the time of day, you know? And who can blame her? Maggie went to school and grew up. I think she always had something like this place in her mind. She was young when she started working at shelters. She lost her aunt a few years back. We're the only family she has now."

Adam finished his coffee and considered her story. "You and Maggie are very close."

"Closer than breathing. I feel like she saved my life. So I look out for her."

"Are you trying to tell me something?"

Delta looked at him closely. "I think you're all right, despite the fact that you're tight with your money. And I know you want her. I'm just wondering what happens after that?"

He frowned. "Are you asking me my intentions?"

"I just want you to know where I stand. I don't want to see Maggie hurt. She's had enough of that in her life." There was a knock at the back door and Delta's face lit up. "That must be Dan."

Adam remembered Dan Rogers from the first night he was there to find Jordan. He shook his hand then made himself scarce. It was clear that Delta and Dan were more than friends.

He wished he knew what was going on between him and Maggie. If *anything* was going on between them. A couple of kisses didn't make a relationship. But he'd be lying if he didn't admit that he was attracted to her open, honest attitude and her sexy legs. She was smart and funny. Her kisses were a surprise to him.

He was still recovering from his short, ugly relationship with Vickie. He needed to be there for Jordan. Any relationship with Maggie Madison was bound to be unpredictable and a lot like stepping into a hurricane. Right now though, it seemed like the only logical thing to do. He wasn't sure if he could convince her or even if he was right but he was serious about trying.

He went back upstairs with a hammer and nails to pound down a few loose boards in the upstairs floor.

Jordan looked at him strangely as she came upstairs. "Uncle Adam? What are you doing here?"

"Some work for the shelter."

"Keeping an eye on me?"

"No. You don't need me to do that, do you?"

"No!" She glanced around them. "I don't think I've ever seen you *not* wearing a suit and tie."

"Everyone changes," he replied. "I'll see you later."

She left him but she kept looking back. Adam smiled and kept pounding. Maybe it was a good thing for her to see him in another light. Maybe he was becoming too stuffy and uptight. Sometimes, on long nights at the office, he thought of himself as Scrooge in his counting house on Christmas Eve. Maybe that meant Maggie was his Jacob Marley. He laughed out loud at that idea and moved on to the next floor repair.

He was working in the basement on another leaky pipe that afternoon when Maggie came running downstairs to find him.

"Thank goodness you're still here! I've got twenty mouths to feed for dinner and the stove stopped working. Could you come and take a look at it?"

Maggie watched him slowly get up. He stretched out his long, lean body from the crouched position he'd been in under the pipe. She probably should have looked away. But that wasn't her style. And he was a lovely sight. Besides, it wasn't like he was naked or something. He was wearing shorts and a t-shirt. *Not that I can't imagine . . .*

He was staring back at her. Maggie's mouth suddenly felt dry. She swallowed hard and forced herself to look away.

"What's wrong with it?" he asked her, amazed and gratified that she'd come to accept his help so quickly.

"What?" Panic seized her. *What was I talking about?*

"The stove?" He smiled at her. "You said the stove wasn't working."

"Uh, yeah. I tried to turn it on but the pilot light went

out and won't re-light. Do you think you can help? I could call someone but it's Sunday. They probably wouldn't come out until Monday."

"I'll see what I can do." His lips twitched. *What in the world was she thinking to have that surprised look on her face?*

"Yeah." Maggie blinked her eyes. "Yeah, that's fine."

"I might have a proposition I'd like to talk to you and Delta about after dinner."

"Really?" Images of her recent fantasies breezed through her mind. "Okay." She smiled at him, her pulse racing. "I'll look forward to it."

Maggie watched Adam as he made a huge pot of chili after getting the pilot to light. She frowned. "What do you think his proposition is?"

Delta was at the table beside her, thinking about Dan and his recent visit. "Huh?"

"Adam told me he has a proposition he wants to talk to us about," Maggie repeated.

"A *proposition,* huh? Sounds like fun. Are you sure he didn't want to talk to you alone?"

"Don't start. I think he really wants to help. Look at him with the kids."

Her friend pried herself away from her own thoughts. "Whatever you think, Maggie. He's been busy here all day, that's for sure. Maybe we could hire him to stand around and fix things all the time."

"What was he doing all day?"

"I don't know. Pounding nails. Drinking coffee."

"Did he say anything to you?"

"Yeah. He said he wanted to get married and have ten children with you!" Delta slumped a little lower on the table.

"You're a big help."

"We were talking about you." Delta's voice was muffled.

"What about me?"

"Adam and I were talking about you being a very nice

young woman who doesn't kiss on the first date, respects her elders and always wears her skirts down below her knee."

"Delta!"

"What?"

"What *really* happened? Or are you making the whole thing up?" Maggie was frustrated with the conversation. What did Adam really say about her?

At that moment, one of the bowls of chili went flying across the table. The boy on the throwing end claimed it was an accident. The girl on the receiving end said he was pestering her the day before, too, would Maggie please ask him to stop?

The girl whose job it was to clean tables that week started crying when she saw the mess. Maggie offered to help her clean it up. Delta settled the rest of the kids down to prevent any further catastrophes.

When all of the kids were finished eating and in the TV room, Adam sat down at one of the picnic style benches beside Delta and Maggie. "How do you do this every day? And why are you still sane?"

"Oh this was a good supper, honey!" Delta assured him. "You just don't know!"

"I don't think I want to know then," Adam stated for the record.

Maggie couldn't hide her curiosity any longer. "What did you want to tell me after dinner?"

"I should clean the kitchen first." He hesitated.

"Don't keep her in suspense any longer," Delta complained. "I don't think I can stand it. We'll help you later."

"You can come, too," he said to Delta. "I think you should be there anyway."

He got to his feet and led the way. "I think I can show you better than telling you."

Behind his back, Delta was waggling her brows at Maggie and whispering, "He's hot for us both!"

Chapter Seven

Maggie nudged her sharply. Delta fell against the wall.

Adam looked at both of them. "Are you okay?"

"Fine." Delta smiled at him. "Just eager to see what you got, sugar."

An hour later, neither woman was sure she wanted to see what he had to show them. They stood behind him and peered at the computer screen over his shoulder. He showed them how badly they were in need of accounting help.

"The money's there," he explained finally. "But your accounts are so screwed up, you can't see it."

Delta was confused. "So let me see if I understand this. We've got an extra ten thousand dollars in the bank that we don't know about because we just keep depositing?"

"And because of these checks you haven't cashed." He held up the group of checks. "I found these in a shoebox. I can create a spreadsheet for you. That way, you can both see what's happening to your money."

"I think we're doing okay without it," Maggie answered offhandedly.

"What are you talking about?" Delta demanded. "You can see what a mess this is. Checks in shoeboxes! We could use his help sorting it out. If he's willing to go through all these boxes and put it all together, I think we should let him do it."

"Excuse us." Maggie drew her friend to the side of the room and whispered, "This is The Ogre, remember?"

"Didn't we agree not to use that while I was here?" Adam prompted, not looking up from the computer screen.

"Sorry," Maggie offered, then, "Do you mind?"

Delta lowered her voice. "Maybe he is. But he's willing to help."

"We don't know him that well. Do we want him involved in our accounting?"

"If he can help, yes!"

"I don't know, Delta."

"Look, this doesn't have to be part of your whole dreamy-eyed thing with him. It could be a business arrangement."

"But he's not an accountant," Maggie argued in a loud whisper. "And there is no dreamy-eyed thing with him."

"I do the accounting for my business. I had two years of accounting in college," he answered like she'd spoken to him.

"Are you listening to us?" Maggie glared at him.

He shrugged and took off his glasses. "It would help if you left the room. I'm not deaf."

"All right!" Maggie was embarrassed that he'd heard their argument over him. She walked out of the room and slammed the door behind her.

"If Maggie isn't comfortable with me doing this—" he began.

"Don't be silly," Delta assured him quickly. "The door just closes easy. She doesn't know her own strength. You go ahead and do your thing, Adam. Let me take care of Maggie."

Adam got ready to leave for the night, packing up his tools and gloves. He'd *thought* it was a good idea to help with the accounting anyway. The problem was that he didn't understand Maggie so he couldn't anticipate anything she was going to do. But his accounting had to be as good as his plumbing and stove repair. He put on his jacket and said goodnight to Jordan before he went home.

"This is a mistake." Delta and Maggie were still arguing about it the next morning.

"The only mistake I see here is not hiring someone before now to keep track of everything. Just think, Maggie, ten thousand dollars! Just think what we could do for this place with that money!"

"We've always kept this kind of stuff between us."

"Us and the United Way and every other agency in this county! It's not like we do something secret here!" Delta faced her. "What are you really afraid of, honey? Is it Adam? Has something else happened between you two?"

Maggie started putting silverware into the dishwasher with unnecessary force. "No, nothing else has happened."

"Is *that* what it is then?"

"No, Delta. It's nothing personal. It's just that I've tried to get money from him all this time. Now he finds we have all this extra money. I feel like an idiot. I can't even keep track of what I've got without asking for more."

"Is that all? Sugar, no man expects a skinny little thing like you to be able to keep track of all those big bad numbers!"

"I don't want to play that game." Maggie pushed a bowl into the sturdy dishwasher. "I'm not an idiot. And I sure don't want to act like an idiot in front of Adam."

"Then just say you made a mistake," Delta continued. "Whatever makes you feel better. The man knows what he's doing. We could use a few pointers. Did you see those checks he found in the shoebox? Maggie, what were those checks doing in the shoebox?"

"I don't know," Maggie conceded. "I guess I was in a hurry one day and forgot."

"And that's why we're in this mess!"

Maggie stuck her tongue out at Delta. She wiped down the cabinets. The familiar clanking sound of the dishwasher faded from her thoughts. Why did it bother her so much that Adam might think she was incompetent? When did she start caring what he thought? He was just another person who needed help. She was spending way too much time thinking about him. She savagely attacked the dirty sink.

It was true that she found Adam attractive. She could

even imagine having some kind of relationship with him. She was flattered that he asked her out. Maybe even excited. Okay, *definitely* excited. She didn't want to feel that way about him. She was pretty sure it couldn't amount to anything. Like every other man in her life, he'd end up discovering that she was too much trouble.

But she couldn't deny that she thought about him that way. He wasn't the ogre she'd imagined. He was a caring uncle. She believed his work around the shelter came from a real desire to help them. His accounting suggestions were probably good, no matter how much they irritated her.

She was just embarrassed, Maggie realized as she wiped down the tables. She was competent. She'd managed to stay in business without his help. But she was careless about her bookkeeping. It wasn't his fault. She was always so busy taking care of everything else that she didn't have time to keep up with all that needed to be done.

A call came in from the free school that there had been a fight between two of the kids from Small Miracles. The free school didn't tolerate fighting or drugs. To keep the opportunity open for all the others, Maggie was ruthless with kids who got in trouble there. She told Delta about the problem then got ready to go.

She was trying to get her car started when Adam drove up to the house. He was dressed, as usual, in a gray suit and a white shirt with a nondescript tie. It didn't matter to her. He was an attractive, sexy man. Why hadn't she ever seen it before?

He stopped by the car. "Having problems?"

"I've got kids fighting at the free school. I can't let that happen." She tried the car again but there was still no response.

"I was dropping off some stuff for Jordan. Need a ride?"

"It'll start."

He waited while she tried the car again. When it still didn't start, he put down Jordan's backpack and took off his gloves. "Open the hood."

Slumping a little in the seat and cursing her car, Maggie pulled the hood lock.

"Try it again," he said from under the hood.

She turned the key but the engine groaned and died. "What now?"

He closed the hood and wiped off his hands. "You give the poor thing a decent burial."

"Adam, it's my car! I depend on it!"

"I'm on my way out, Maggie. I can take you with me. That's the best I can do right now."

"What will I do later?"

"Get a good mechanic."

She hit the steering wheel. "I can't believe this!"

"Come on," he coaxed her. "I promise not to talk to you since you're in a bad mood."

Maggie got out of her car and slammed the door. She stormed after him to his car. "I'm not in a bad mood!"

"No?"

"No. I'm a little upset, but I'm not in a bad mood."

Adam opened the door for her. "Okay."

"What does *that* mean?"

"It means okay. If you say you're not in a bad mood, you're not in a bad mood."

"But you don't agree with me?"

"Do I always have to agree with you? That's what drives you to ask me for donations after I've said no a million times, isn't it? Everyone has to agree with Maggie Madison!"

Maggie got in the old Mercedes and slammed the door shut. She glared at Adam. "People don't *always* have to agree with me."

He started to argue with her then took a look at her mutinous face. He smiled instead. "What's wrong?"

"What do you mean?" She huffed. "My car won't start!"

He turned in the seat to face her. "I know from personal experience that it takes more than that to get you down. I've slammed the door in your face ten times and you still came back for more."

Those memories didn't help. "It's nothing."

"You feel stupid because I found that lost money, don't you?"

She folded her arms across her chest. "I don't want to talk about that."

"I was only trying to help." He stroked a finger along her arm.

Maggie moved her arm and started talking to cover up her uneasiness with him. "I know. Jazzy's mother came for her yesterday. We barely managed to keep her here while her mother got straightened out. She doesn't want to leave but I don't have any choice. I know she'll be back."

"That doesn't sound good," he sympathized, tucking a strand of her hair behind her ear.

"And that was on top of Megan's mother coming here drunk to find her and take her home. She's six years old, Adam. We found her living in a car."

"Can't you stop her?"

Maggie was slowly sliding closer to him as she spoke. She didn't realize until she looked up and found that she was already in the circle of his open arms. "No. Not for long anyway."

"I'm sorry, Maggie." He kissed her forehead and drew her closer to him. "I think your heart's too soft for this job."

"Sometimes, I think it's my head that's too soft." Her forehead tingled where he kissed it. It was just a sympathy kiss. Something a friend might do. But it felt so good being held against him. She could feel his heart beating. His warmth seeped into her making her vision a little blurred around the edges. This was definitely not a friendship thing.

"But you have the heart of a champion, don't you?" He marveled at her resilience and energy. "You keep trying."

"I always keep trying," she murmured, snuggling closer to him without allowing herself to think about what she was doing. "You know that."

"I do." He kissed her cheek then raised her hair to kiss the side of her neck. "Mmm, you smell good."

"Soap," she confessed in a soft voice.

"I like soap." His lips grazed hers.

Maggie sighed and relaxed against him. It was the easiest thing to be with Adam. At least this way. They might argue about things but they were good at this part. Who would've guessed?

Adam's kisses were slow and patient. It was the same way he talked to her. As though he had all the time in the world. There was nothing else to do but sit there and kiss her. He was good at focusing on one thing or one person. Maggie envied him that ability. She was always too scattered.

"Is something else wrong?" he asked.

"No." She wrapped her arms around his neck and kissed him again. "I was just unfocused."

He put his head back to look into her face. "I've never known a woman like you, Maggie."

Her eyes narrowed. "Is that a good or a bad thing?"

"A good thing," he assured her, smoothing down a fly-away length of her hair. "I didn't realize that you had this fire in you, this passion. Otherwise I would've given up fighting you a long time ago. How could I hope to hold out against you?"

"You can't. But now you know the truth."

"What's that?"

"That I've been throwing money into shoeboxes and going out for more. I've been asking you for money I should've known was there. I feel like an idiot."

He kissed her lightly. "Is that what you're worried about? Maggie, there's no way I could doubt your sincerity after spending this time with you. You're a bad bookkeeper but that just means you need help. I can get you started but you need to hire an accountant for the shelter."

She bit her lip. "You mean you don't think I'm an idiot?"

"I think you're amazing." He kissed her. "Beautiful." He kissed her again, lingering to savor her sweetness. "Courageous." Any other words to describe her were lost in the feel and taste of her.

"Stop teasing!" She wrapped her arms around his neck and pulled him down, close enough to see the flecks of gold in his eyes.

Adam lost track of time and place. All he could think about was her. There was a knocking sound that slowly invaded his consciousness. He opened his eyes with difficulty, forcing himself back to reason. The windows were steamed over. *I'm sitting in my car outside the shelter, making out with Maggie. And there's someone at the door!*

"Maggie? Are you in there?" Delta's voice penetrated the haze that surrounded them. She pounded on the door again. "Maggie?"

Maggie whispered, "Delta!"

"Just pull your jacket on." Adam helped her as he tried to right his tie and shirt.

Maggie finally gave up arranging her clothing and pulled her coat shut. She looked at Adam. His hair was completely messed up. His lips were swollen from her kisses. Her cheeks were hot from the heat they'd generated.

"Maggie?" Delta called again. "Are you okay?"

Adam rolled down the window a crack, enough to see Delta's concerned face. "Hi Delta."

"Hi yourself." Delta looked at Maggie. "I thought you were going to the free school?"

"The car wouldn't start," Maggie defended. "Adam is giving me a ride."

Delta smiled. "I can see that, sugar! I was just wondering when you were gonna make it to the school! I was afraid the car was running and you'd both die of asphyxiation out here. Dan came in and he didn't know if he should hose you down or use the Jaws of Life!"

"Go away," Maggie told her impatiently. "We're leaving now."

"Good thing. A crowd is starting to gather and I think I saw the Channel 6 news truck."

Adam rolled up the window and started the car. "Which way to the free school?"

"It's about five miles up on Charter Street." Maggie kept

up a running conversation all the way to the school. She didn't care that Adam didn't say anything. She put her clothes in place and brushed her hair. She avoided talking about what happened between them. Or the idea of them going out on a date. She wasn't going to bring it up if he didn't. He might've changed his mind, despite the kisses.

Adam didn't mind. He didn't want to talk about it either. What was wrong with him? One minute they were talking and the next, they were making out in a car like two teenagers. He was just glad Jordan wasn't there to see it. He was acting in the same irresponsible manner that he was always yelling at her about.

"I can wait for you." He stopped the car at the school that was located in an old grocery store.

"No thanks," Maggie decided. "I don't know how long it will take. I'll take the bus back. I'm sure you have better things to do than sit around and wait for me."

"Okay. I'll see you later."

Maggie was a little surprised and unhappy when he didn't insist on staying. On one hand, she didn't want to argue about it. On the other hand, she probably would've given in and let him take her back to the shelter. She was such a mess.

Aunt Leila always said: If you didn't put it all upfront, how could a person know what to do? Even worse, maybe she'd talked so much about completely ridiculous things that he just wanted her out of the car. Or maybe he was worried that she'd bring up the date again. Maybe he was regretting the offer.

She couldn't help it. She walked into the school thinking about Adam instead of the two boys she was there for. Adam was wrong for her. He was too serious. She was sure he'd want some kind of committed relationship. That was something she never considered. At least not seriously. Her choice of lifestyle didn't allow it. She was happy that way. She liked to go out and have a good time but she didn't want a permanent person in her life. It was too complicated. No one ever stayed around that long.

Then suddenly she wasn't so sure. It was nice settling back into his arms and telling him about what was wrong. It was tantalizing to think it could always be that way. Her emotions were at war with her logic. Logic and experience told her that relationships never worked out. Her heart was whispering "maybe."

"Hi Maggie." The principal of the free school interrupted her thoughts. "I have the two boys in here."

She spent the next two hours trying to convince the principal that the boys shouldn't lose their places at the school. It was customary for the free-school to suspend anyone who was caught fighting. The principal was willing to make an exception because both boys had recently been abandoned. It was their last and final warning. Anything else, even the slightest problem, would terminate them at the free school. There was no board to appeal to or higher authority. The principal's word was law.

The boys were sent back to the shelter for the day. Maggie rode home with the pair on the bus. They were the same boys, Kevin and Robbie, who'd been fighting Sunday.

Maggie touched her cheek gingerly, recalling that incident. "Would one of you like to tell me what the problem is now?"

Neither boy looked at her.

"I don't hear anything. You're both using up your chances at the school and at the shelter. I know neither one of you wants to go back on the street."

"He started it," Robbie relented.

"That is so lame!" Kevin retorted.

"Could one of you tell me what happened?" Maggie put herself between them.

Both boys stared at her without answering.

"What could be worth losing your places at the shelter *and* in the free school?" A light bulb turned on in her head. "A girl? It's a girl, isn't it?"

"My girl," Robbie growled at Kevin.

"She don't see it that way," Kevin replied.

"If you keep acting like idiots," Maggie cautioned, "she's not going to be with either of you!"

"You don't get it," Robbie told her. "You're too old to understand what makes a man feel special about a woman."

Kevin glanced at her. "See? He can't even talk right."

"I think he said what he wanted to say without any problem," Maggie assured him despite the fact that Robbie said she was old.

"You ain't *that* old," Robbie said. "And you're good looking anyway. You don't got to worry."

"Thanks." Maggie changed the conversation back to their problem instead of her age. They talked all the way back to the shelter. They didn't completely agree but they did agree to let the girl make the choice. They shook hands and got off the bus. Maggie felt sorry for the girl, whoever she was. She was going to have to decide between the two.

Dan and Adam were at the shelter when she got back. She'd missed the fireworks when Jazzy's mother came back for her, this time with her new boyfriend.

"Thank goodness they were here!" Delta greeted her. "I called social services but they couldn't send someone out until tomorrow. I swear I think that man had a gun!"

Dan laughed. "I don't think so, Delta. He was just scared."

Maggie took off her coat. "So what happened with Jazzy?"

"Ronnie said she was going to get a lawyer to take her from you. Then she left," Adam answered. "I know it isn't much. But it's a reprieve."

"It's the best we can do." Maggie sighed. "Is Jazzy back from school yet?"

Delta looked puzzled. "The other kids are home. I didn't notice her coming in. I probably just missed her. Unless you think something happened."

"I hope not," Maggie muttered, heading for the stairs.

She took the stairs two at a time. There was no sign of Jazzy. The girls who shared her room said her mother picked her up at the free school. Probably while Maggie was busy with Kevin and Robbie. She kicked at a stray soccer ball when she got back out in the hall. "I hate losing a kid that way!"

"They must've gone right from here to the school," Delta theorized.

"Not everybody has a happy ending, Maggie," Dan told her plainly. "You've been here long enough to know that."

"Yeah." She slapped the old banister. "I know. But it doesn't mean I have to like it."

"She's fine." Delta took Maggie's arm. "We've been through this a dozen times. It happens."

"A dozen times too many," Maggie agreed, still angry.

"I think we should come down here and start lunch. Macaroni and cheese always cheers you up," Delta said pleasantly.

"I have to go on duty," Dan said, looking at his watch.

"And I have to get back to work," Adam added.

"We're used to doing it alone, thanks anyway," Delta told Dan with a tart edge to her voice.

"Honey." Dan maneuvered Delta away from Maggie's side and into the pantry in the kitchen. "Don't sound that way."

Maggie took a seat at one of the tables.

Adam sat beside her. "I can go in later, if it'll help."

"Thanks. But Dan's right. I'll get over it. I always do," Maggie said quietly. "You don't have to worry anyway. A new kid will take her place. Delta and Dan will work things out. Life will go on here. It always does."

Adam tried to divine if she was happy or angry about that fact. He gave up after a few minutes of looking at the side of her face. He glanced at the pantry and changed the subject. "I can imagine running this place would make a relationship hard."

"I'm sure it would."

"But you haven't tried so you don't know?"

"I don't *want* to try so I don't know," Maggie answered. That wasn't strictly true, but she wasn't in any mood to consider the possibilities.

"You must be the only woman in the world that doesn't want any kind of relationship. Doesn't it get lonely?"

"Not as lonely as if you trust someone to be there and they don't stay with you," she told him seriously. "I'd rather expect the worst."

"Maggie, some relationships are good." Adam couldn't believe those words came out of his mouth.

"Oh? Have you had one?"

"No."

"Then how do you know?"

"My parents were married for forty three years when my mother died," Adam said. "My father never remarried. He was in love with her until the day he died. I know it can be complicated but it *does* happen."

"What are the chances? One in a million?"

"I think it happens more often than that." Adam was defending this idea even as he argued it out in his own mind.

"What about you?" she asked him. "Why haven't you been out there trying to find another relationship?"

"I have my work and Jordan to consider. That makes it more complicated."

Maggie laughed grimly. "In other words, you don't think it's possible either. Maybe it happened for your parents but it hasn't happened for you."

Adam didn't answer.

She got to her feet and went to knock on the pantry door. "Delta, lunch!"

Delta and Dan came out of the pantry with their clothes wrinkled and their eyes dazed.

"So, you'll call later?" Delta asked him.

"I will," Dan promised and kissed her again.

"I have to get back to work." Adam slipped out the door and got in his car. He didn't leave right away.

Why was he trying to convince Maggie that relationships worked between two people? Since when did he believe in happily ever after? And even if he did in some little corner of his heart, why would he try to convince Maggie of it?

He wasn't in a good position to offer her a relationship. Not with the painful fragments of his last try still giving him splinters in his backside. And maybe he owed it to Jordan not to get involved with anyone yet. There were still too many loose ends that needed to be tied together.

Maggie was a gorgeous woman. All that creamy skin and those big blue eyes. He liked the way her mind worked. He admired her open, generous heart. He enjoyed kissing her, too. Being with her was like a jolt of high energy shooting through him. It was enough to melt even his frost-bitten heart. He wanted to believe something was possible with her. His heart wanted him to take that chance even if his mind wasn't sure.

He was about to start the car when a shout from inside the house caught his attention. A group of kids came running out of the house into the cold afternoon. Adam took his keys out of the ignition and ran into the house.

He looked around but didn't see anyone. He heard shouting from upstairs. Two boys ran down the stairs and out of the door. "Where's Maggie and Delta?"

"Upstairs!"

Adam skirted the scared children as they came down. He saw Jordan with the two boys who'd been fighting the night before. "Have you seen Maggie?"

"She ran into the bathroom with Delta," Jordan told him. "Uncle Adam, this is Kevin and this is Robbie."

He barely acknowledged them, although he did notice Robbie's arm around Jordan's waist. He heard Maggie's voice in his head. *"She's a young woman now."* He gritted his teeth and went down the hallway to the bathroom.

Megan was standing at the bathroom door. She looked up at him with frightened eyes. "I didn't mean to do it."

He crouched down beside her. "Do what, sweetie?"

Her brown eyes were enormous in her pale face. "I didn't mean to make the toilet fall through the floor."

Chapter Eight

Adam walked cautiously into the bathroom and looked at the place where the toilet should have been. There was nothing but a gaping hole in the floor. Water sluiced down the wall from the pipe that had been connected to it. "Let's stay out of the bathroom and close the door for now. I'm going downstairs to see what happened."

He found Maggie and Delta in the basement with the missing toilet. They were both soaked. Water was spraying out of two different pipes. "Do you have a wrench?"

"I couldn't find it," Maggie told him, wiping water from her face.

"We thought maybe we could close it off before we have to build an ark." Delta pushed her wet hair back out of her face.

"We have to find the main tap. It should be down here." He slogged through the knee deep water until he found it. It wouldn't turn by hand. He found a wrench and shut the main line off. Water still dripped from the ceiling. It would take some time to dry out the basement but the flood was over. "I think this is more than a basic plumbing problem."

Maggie grimaced. "There goes some of that extra money."

Adam rescued a box of sneakers from the flood. "I think you should consider getting a new shelter."

"Yeah, we will when pigs grow wings," Delta retorted.

He looked around at the rotting timbers beneath the bottom floor. "Seriously. We could set up a fundraiser for the shelter. You already have a head start on the money. People love to give to charitable causes."

"We could build a bigger house. Lord knows we could use a bigger place with more bathrooms." Delta was starting to get into the idea.

"That would take a lot of money," Maggie said realistically, but she was willing to listen. "What kind of fundraiser?

"Something big and bold," Adam began to explain. "Something that will make everyone take notice. The Chamber of Commerce had a big Mardi Gras night a few years ago that brought in almost a million dollars."

"A million?" Delta squeaked as she looked at Maggie. "We wouldn't even need that much."

Adam continued, "And once we start the promotion and let people know why we're having the fundraiser, we'll probably have people donating land to put it on."

"You're a genius!" Delta put her arms around his neck and kissed him.

"How do we start?" Maggie asked wishing she'd thought of that move first.

"I'd say first, we call a plumber and a carpenter to take care of this mess."

"Adam." Maggie began to think about the enormous project he was instigating. "We don't have any experience with something this big. Should we look for someone like the person who organized the Mardi Gras thing for the Chamber? How will we know what to do?"

He smiled at her. "I did the Mardi Gras for the Chamber, Maggie. I'll be glad to organize this for you."

At that moment, Maggie was sure she was in love. With the *idea*, of course; not with *Adam!*

The fundraiser idea was pushed back while Delta and Maggie negotiated for the repairs to the shelter. They threatened the plumber who was supposed to have fixed the pipes and the toilet. That got them half off on the work and a quick fix on the toilet. But the carpenter was expensive.

"We've only got twenty-five-hundred left out of that ten thousand," Delta told her partner after breakfast. "I don't know if the fundraiser is possible."

Maggie didn't respond. She was cleaning up the kitchen after the meal. She and Delta split the chore that morning while they waited for Adam to make some phone calls.

"Are you listening to me?"

"Yes. I'm just thinking about other things," Maggie finally responded.

"What other things are more important than this?"

"Adam and Jordan have their first session of family counseling today. Jordan's been here five days and I don't see any sign that she's getting ready to move out."

Delta didn't understand. "Isn't that a good thing? We don't want her to leave yet. Her father *is* helping us plan for the fundraiser."

"I'm sure his niece didn't live with the president of the Chamber of Commerce while he was planning the Mardi Gras."

"What's up with you? You've been like a hornet before winter, looking for somebody to sting."

Maggie didn't want to elaborate on the great care she'd taken not to be alone with Adam for the past week. Five long days of knowing he was wandering from one end of the shelter to another. She planned every step so that she didn't find herself alone with him. Trying to stay away from him so she wouldn't be miserable was making her whole life a nightmare. She didn't know what was worse. Falling into his arms every time she saw him or worrying about it.

Either way, Adam was becoming important in her life. Being involved with him and the fundraiser was making it harder. There were long moments during the day when she imagined the two of them together. "I'm just looking forward to my night off. I'm going to go out and not come back until sunrise."

"I know you, Maggie Madison. I can see behind that fake smile and all that activity. You're worried about something. Is it still that child whose mother took her back?"

Losing Jazzy still bothered her, it wasn't a lie. Maggie latched on to that excuse with lightning speed. "I can't help it, Delta. I just can't get over it."

"You *do* need a night off!"

"Who's getting a night off?" Adam asked as he walked into the kitchen for coffee.

" 'Bye, Uncle Adam." Jordan kissed him as she ran for her bus. Kevin and Robbie were both right behind her.

Maggie watched them. Suddenly, she knew who was causing the trouble between the two boys. Jordan!

"Tonight is Maggie's monthly night off," Delta announced in an obvious way.

Adam put on his coat. He considered his words carefully. It was obvious that Maggie was avoiding him. He thought it was probably a good idea. He couldn't believe Jordan didn't want to go home. He found himself lying in his bed every night, thinking about Maggie and why they probably shouldn't be together. The condo was too empty and quiet. He usually ended up on his computer until dawn.

He knew it might be a mistake. She hadn't given him any hint of wanting to spend time alone with him in the last few days. But the words were going to come out anyway. No amount of self-discipline could keep them back. "Maybe we could have dinner."

Delta smiled like a big possum. "Now, that sounds like a good idea. Doesn't it Maggie?"

"I, uh—"

Adam felt like an idiot. *I should've known better!* "Of course if you have other plans . . ."

"Plans?" Delta closed up that loophole before Maggie could grab it. "She doesn't ever have plans. Half of the time she hangs around here on her night off. It would be good for her to get out, wouldn't it, honey?"

Maggie wanted to find the appropriate response to Delta's suggestion but her brain went blank. She smiled at

Adam while she searched for a logical reason that she couldn't go out with him.

Adam saw the struggle. He realized that she was as wary of him as he was of her. He'd been right. Avoiding him for the last week had been deliberate. It stung his ego a little. Except when he considered *why* she'd gone to all that trouble to avoid him. He still wanted to see her, spend some time alone with her. He wanted to hold her again and . . . "Let's say seven?"

Maggie opened her mouth but no words came out. Instead she thought about how much she liked the sound of his voice. Her knees felt weak. She knew she'd already lost the battle. "We have the first family counseling session today."

He smiled. "I know. Four, right?"

"Right." *I love his eyes. I love the way he looks at me.*

"But that shouldn't go on for more than an hour, should it?"

"Right." Her brain was feeling a little mushy and her face was flushed.

"Then I'll pick you up at seven."

"Okay." She agreed with a breathless quality to her voice that made her want to scream. If he'd called her on the phone, she could've said no. She felt very sure about that. But face-to-face, it was hard to look into those beautiful eyes, see him smile, and say no to anything.

She admitted it. She was weak. All she could think about was what happened the last time they were alone together. That's why she was avoiding him. That's why she wanted to kill Delta for standing there smiling and waving as Adam left. "Why did you do that?"

"Because you're too stubborn to do it for yourself."

"You know how I feel about relationships." Maggie cleaned a broad swath of table space that was covered with syrup.

"How do you know he wants a relationship? Has he proposed or something? Was that what he was doing when you two were in that car all steamed up and—"

"The man has relationship written all over him, Delta! Don't be stupid. Look at you. You were married. You can't wait to go back and do it again. That's the way people are who've been in relationships."

"And you're calling me stupid? That man has been burned. I think he's as nervous as you! And let me tell you something else, stick girl, marriage to the right man is the best thing that can happen to a woman! If I didn't think Dan and I had the chance to be *half* as happy as Matt and I were, I wouldn't be fooling around with him. What's wrong with you?"

"Delta, you know—"

"That your parents weren't happy together and your father left when your mother died. Blah. Blah. Blah. That's ancient history! Wake up! Girls with skinny legs like yours don't have men falling all over them every day."

"He isn't falling all over me."

"Of course not, you're too busy avoiding him!" Delta got up from her chair. "I have people to call about permits for the fundraiser. Give him a chance, Maggie. Maybe he just wants to have a good time. Maybe he'd rather die than marry you!"

Maggie finished with the kitchen. She was excited about going out with Adam that night. Her stomach felt like she was coming down from the top of a roller coaster. There had to be some way to deal with it. She went to her room and read through everything she'd accumulated about the Fuentes' family. Reviewing all the problems he and Jordan had would throw some cold water on that excitement, if anything would. But the papers trembled in her hand and her mind wandered.

Get a grip!

She forced herself to focus on her notes. She'd already had some counseling sessions with Jordan. She hadn't tried to talk to Adam. But she knew that Jordan was leaning heavily towards going to live with her great aunt in Vancouver. It sounded glamorous and exciting to the girl. She didn't try to talk her out of it. That wasn't her job.

Despite Adam's doubts about his parenting skills, she knew he'd be crushed if Jordan went away. If it happened, Adam might feel she helped Jordan make that decision. Part of her cringed at that idea. Her personal involvement with the family made it impossible for her to be objective.

Maggie threw down her notes and walked around her room. She was too close, too involved. They needed to talk to a stranger. Jordan flatly refused to talk to anyone but her. It couldn't possibly end well. Adam was bound to be hostile. Who could blame him? He thought he might be doing what was best for Jordan by sending her away. But he loved her and he had no other family. Life without her was going to be hard.

She didn't need this frustration. Who'd have thought that The Ogre would be more of a problem helping the shelter than ignoring it? Who'd have thought he'd kiss like an angel? Or that she wouldn't be able to say no to him when he asked her out, even though she knew it was a mistake.

She'd made a promise to herself as soon as she was old enough to understand what happened between her parents. She wasn't going to make the same mistake her parents made. There wasn't any man worth a life of desperation and unhappiness. She was better off alone.

She looked at the wall of photographs in her bedroom. There was a picture of almost every child who'd lived in the shelter. She could remember all of their names. Most of them overcame terrible things to make a better life for themselves. They were her family. Delta was her family. She didn't need anyone else.

Delta knocked on the door. "Mail."

Maggie opened the door and took the envelope from her. It was postmarked from St. Louis. A feeling of dread gripped her.

"Secret friend?"

"Yeah. Too secret for even me to know about it." Maggie opened the envelope to a page of large, scrawling words.

Delta tried to read the letter. "Who's it from?"

Maggie crushed the paper in her hand then tossed it into the trash. "My father."

"Your father? Why'd you throw it away?"

"He's going to be in town. He wants to see me. It happens every couple of years."

"Maggie, I think I kind of took for granted that he was *dead*. You didn't tell me he was still alive?"

"There's a reason for that, Delta. As far as I'm concerned, he *is* dead."

"That's harsh."

"I know."

They sat beside each other on her bed. Delta put her arm around Maggie's shoulders. "He wants to see you?"

"Yes."

"You should see him, honey! He's your blood, you know? Nothing can take away from that."

"He abandoned me, Delta. Why should I see him now? I don't need him anymore."

"Because you've still got issues. Can't you see that? Why do you think you're so worked up about it? Of course you still need him!"

"I wanted to see him when I was Jordan's age," Maggie replied. "I don't want to see him now."

"How'd he know where to find you anyway?"

"The last time, he saw an article about me working with homeless kids."

Delta didn't press the issue any further. She hugged Maggie tightly then smiled and kissed her cheek. "I think you should reconsider. But if you can't, I guess you can't. He'll be gone one day and it'll be too late. I wish I could have my mama or daddy back again for even five minutes."

"I know you do. But this is different."

Delta looked at the notes on her bed. "You working on the Fuentes thing?"

"Yeah. No matter how I look at it, it looks bad."

"Refer them to someone else after today," Delta said. "You know you're too close to do a good job."

"You're right. I wouldn't do it this time but they have to start somewhere. And Jordan won't talk to anyone else yet. I'm going to refer them to someone else after this session. I'm in over my head."

"Because you got feelings for that man, right?"

"I wouldn't call them feelings exactly."

"Don't tell me you were makin' out with him in that car for shelter money?"

"*Delta!*"

"You know I'm teasing you! You're an emotional mess, girl! You need to take some time off."

"I know. But someone made other arrangements for me tonight."

Delta snapped her fingers. "Tell him you can't go. Tell him you don't need a night out with a gorgeous man who thinks you're hot. You need a night with a hot bath and some double chocolate ice cream."

"Maybe I'll do that."

"You know I'm teasing!" Delta said. "You want to go out with him. Just do it. Take the chance."

Maggie laughed at her friend's quick turnaround. "Is the bathroom finished yet?"

"Yep. It looks good, too. I'm on my way downstairs to start lunch. Want to come along?"

Delta took Adam into the family room and got him some iced tea while Maggie waited in the kitchen. She was talking to Jordan. "This is going to be the only joint counseling session you can have here with me."

"Why? I like you, Maggie." She wiggled her eyebrows. "And Uncle Adam *really* likes you."

"Are you okay with that idea, Jordan? Your uncle said you had some problems when he had the relationship with Vickie."

"At first," Jordan told her. "Now, it doesn't matter. Now I want to go live in Canada and get to know my mom's family. I want to know Uncle Adam is happy after I leave."

Maggie glanced up at her. "Trying to make yourself feel better about leaving him?"

"You don't have to make it sound like I won't ever see him again! I'll see him during school breaks and on holidays."

"But you won't be part of his life anymore like you are now. Are you sure that's what you want?"

"I'm sure."

Maggie closed her notebook. "Okay. Because once the decision is made, it won't be easy to reverse."

"What do you mean?"

"Once they change your school and get you set up there, your mother's family will want you to stay. Then you'll be pulled in another direction."

"That's not what I want!" Jordan told her passionately. "I want to be free."

"Okay. I hope you consider what you want very carefully." Maggie got her notes together and stood up. "Here we go."

The session only lasted about a half an hour. At that point, Jordan declared that she was finished with counseling.

Adam took a deep breath. "This is an impossible situation. If we're going to get help as a family, we need to do it somewhere else."

Jordan didn't want to hear it. "But Maggie—"

"—is very good at what she does," he finished for her. "She was good enough to take you in here even though she doesn't have the room and you don't really need her help. We don't have to make this any harder for her, do we?"

Jordan looked past him to the picture on the wall. "I want to go to Vancouver."

"We've gone through this before."

"I want to get to know my mother's family," Jordan argued. "They'll understand me."

"It will be different than living here," Adam reminded

her. "And if I sign over custody to them, there's no coming back except for visits."

"You can't hold on to me forever," Jordan accused him. "You never want me to go out and have any fun. You don't want to do anything with me. You don't have time for it!"

"Jordan!" Adam called after her as she ran out of the room.

"I'm sorry." Maggie got to her feet, feeling awkward and useless. "I have the names of several very good counselors who'd be glad to see both of you."

"Thanks." He took the list and stood up beside her. "I'm sorry, too, Maggie. I meant what I said about what you've done for Jordan."

"I really think she's saying these things to get your attention. I've talked with her a few times. I don't think she really wants to live in Canada. She wants to be with you. You work a lot of hours and she thinks you're ignoring her for your job."

"I work a lot of hours because I have to work a lot of hours," he defended. "Jordan has to understand that it takes money to buy her clothes and concert tickets."

"Maybe she could do with less if she had more of your time."

He ran a hand through his hair. "Maggie, I'm sure you mean well. But I don't think you understand the problem."

She tossed down her notebook. "And this is why you need someone else to suggest things to you. Everything *I* suggest is wrong in your mind, and suspect in Jordan's eyes."

"I don't think everything you say is wrong!"

"No? Wouldn't you at least pause to *think* about a suggestion if it came from a *different* qualified therapist? You don't have enough confidence in me to gain anything from what I say."

He didn't answer.

Maggie took that for agreement. Stung, she went one step further. "And I don't think we should go out tonight. I'm more than just big eyes and short skirts. I know I haven't always acted like it with you and that's my fault. I'm not good with computers and accounting. But I am good at understanding people. You and I are too different. We could never want the same things."

Adam wasn't sure what to say. It was like the world had gone haywire. This thing with Jordan had thrown him off. The idea of dating Maggie Madison would have been laughable the day before Jordan ran away. He didn't agree with everything Maggie said but maybe it was time to refocus. He was acting like an idiot; sitting in cars making out, rolling around in the trash with her. "All right."

She nodded, biting her lip.

"I guess I'll go and see where Jordan's going."

"That's probably a good idea." Maggie played around with her notebook and pen until he left the room. She looked at the brightly colored furniture and wanted to throw it all through the window. Delta was right. She needed a night to herself.

Three hours later, Maggie wished she'd made other plans. She couldn't separate herself from what was going on inside the shelter. She sat in her room with the door closed but it didn't help. She picked up a torrid romance novel she'd been trying to get through for a while. But every time someone yelled or there was a thump, she threw down the book and got to her feet.

She jumped up when she heard a loud crashing sound. It was followed by Delta's voice organizing the kids into cleaning up whatever it was. She sat back down again but it was too late. There was no way to relax.

She paced her bedroom for a while. She was going to have to go out even if she spent her time at an all night café. She looked at her worn, faded jeans and wooly purple sweater. They would do. She put on her socks and boots, slipped her arms into her coat then opened the door.

Adam was on the threshold raising his hand to knock. "Maggie!"

"Adam?"

"I was wrong. I think *we* were wrong. At least about this part. Let's go out somewhere. Jordan's working on a paper for history. She's in for the night. I don't care what happened this afternoon. The counseling is separate. Let's go out together somewhere."

She considered his invitation. "Well, I wasn't—"

He glanced significantly at her jacket. "Don't tell me you weren't going out. If you don't want to go out with me, just say so."

"It's very complicated."

"It doesn't have to be, Maggie. Let's just go out."

"Out where?" She stalled for time. Her heart was racing. She had knots in her stomach. It didn't matter that she'd spent all afternoon convincing herself that she *didn't* want to see him unless she was asking him for a donation for the shelter.

"Anywhere. It doesn't matter," he answered. "You pick a place."

"I'm not dressed to go out somewhere decent."

"Maggie Madison, are you backing down from a fight?"

His sexy eyes challenged her. And his lips . . . she bit her own in protest to remind herself that she *really* didn't want to kiss him again. He didn't have any respect for her or her opinions. He didn't understand her. He was a huge mistake just waiting to break her heart. She needed to be strong. She should stay away from him.

But she was weak. "What time do you want to go?"

He smiled at her after consulting his watch. "How about now?"

The smile did her in. "Okay. But I need ten minutes."

"Why? You look fine."

"Give me ten minutes and I'll look better."

"Okay. Ten minutes. Then I'm coming in after you."

She closed the door in his face. Adam slumped against the wall. He thought some of his business dealings were tense but nothing like this! His heart was pounding and his hands were shaking. But he was actually going out with Maggie. It was crazy to come and ask her after she made it so clear that she didn't want to see him. But the idea wouldn't let go of him.

He didn't want to think about whether it was right or wrong. He just wanted to be alone with her for a while. Okay, not alone. They'd probably be out at a restaurant or something. But it would be somewhere away from the shelter and the problems they both faced. He wanted to listen to her voice, look in her eyes, and see her smile. Was that too much to ask?

He looked down at himself and realized that he could do with a change, too. It took only seven minutes to get ready. He changed out of his suit coat and slacks and pulled on a pair of jeans he'd bought that morning after he asked her out. He snatched a tan sweater from his briefcase and threw it over his head. He combed his hair then sat in the kitchen to tie the laces on his new tennis shoes. He could hear the kids in the hall clamoring for the TV.

Jordan met him there. "You really like her, huh?"

"Are you okay with that?"

"Not that it's any of my business." She shrugged. "But I think Maggie's nice. You two would be good together."

Adam smiled at his suddenly mature niece. "Thanks. We'll probably just talk about you."

"Yeah. You dressed up to go out and talk about me, right?"

"Probably," he replied. "You know, it's been a long time since you and I went out together."

"I'm too old for you to take out to Chucky Cheese's, Uncle Adam."

"What about somewhere else?"

"Think you'd have time?" She looked skeptical.

Maggie's words from that afternoon bit him hard. "I always have time for you, Jordan. I love you."

She looked away from him, scribbling in her notebook. "Maybe sometime we can go out together when I'm here on vacation from Canada. I guess we'll see."

He stood up, trying not to feel defeated. *Patience.* "How do I look?"

"Like someone else's uncle." She stared at his jeans. "Where'd you get those?"

"Why? Is something wrong with them?"

"The only thing wrong with them is that *you're* in them!" She laughed. "You know, Maggie might think you're kind of cool for an old guy."

He laughed and kissed her. "I hope so. Good night, Jordan."

"Good night. Have a good time."

Maggie stepped out of her room. She squirmed in the plain gray skirt that came down past her knees. It was tight, adhering to every curve of her body. The six-inch split on the left side was its only embellishment. It felt awkward to have that much material on her legs without wearing pants. But she was trying to show Adam that she wasn't all about short skirts and purple tights. She was wearing Delta's blue blouse that was lacy and . . . nice. It reminded her of something her aunt would have worn.

"Nine minutes and thirty seconds," Adam said as she joined him. "Time to spare."

Maggie looked at him in his jeans and sweater. She couldn't believe it. "What are you wearing?"

"Jordan said the same thing." He was beginning to get annoyed. "Is it me or the jeans?"

"Both! I've never seen you in anything except gray suits and ties! I didn't think you owned anything else."

"I didn't until I asked you out. And look at you." He held her hand as he returned the intimate survey. "I can't even see your knees!"

"Yeah, well, don't get used to it," she replied awkwardly. "I'd hate to have to hit the streets looking for a kid like this."

"You look beautiful," he assured her. "Just different."

"I guess I could say the same for you."

If he wasn't wearing those stiff new jeans and tennis shoes, she might have turned around and gone back into her room. But he'd made the effort and so could she. Besides, he looked pretty good like that.

"Are you wearing your coat?" he asked a second time as they stopped in front of the back door.

Maggie almost walked into him. She was too busy admiring his long legs and broad shoulders to pay attention to what he was saying. "Uh-yeah, thanks."

He held the coat for her and she slipped her arms into it. His hands lingered a moment too long, sliding across her shoulders after it was in place. She closed her eyes and relaxed against him, breathing in the warm, clean, male smell of him. It made her vividly recall what it was like being close to him in the car.

"I love the way you smell," he whispered, nuzzling the soft skin just behind her ear.

"I love the way you do that," she answered in an unsteady voice.

A trio of eight-year-olds ran through the kitchen. Adam moved away from her. "I think we should go."

"I've been thinking that for a few hours," she agreed with a big smile plastered across her face.

Chapter Nine

Maggie figured he'd drive. Instead he suggested that they walk along the quiet street. It was cold but dry. There was a large white moon illuminating the sidewalks. The lighted buildings of downtown Atlanta added to the glow. They walked past Centennial Park and watched the water jets fly into the air. They didn't talk about Jordan or Vickie, the shelter, or his business.

"I always wanted to be an astronaut," Adam told her as they walked and looked up at the moon. "I knew I couldn't be one but I wanted to."

"Why didn't you think you could be one?"

"Because I knew I had to work with my father." He shrugged. "I accepted it from a very early age."

"What about your brother? Didn't he help out?"

"Yes. But I was the oldest. It was up to me to help my father." He looked down at her. "What about you?"

"I told you that my father left me when my mother died. My Aunt Leila was very strict, very prim. She had very definite ways of doing things. She was good to me. I never thought she didn't love me."

"And that made you resent your father even more?"

"I suppose so," she half agreed. "I wanted him to come back for me and take me away from those white gloves and cleaning under my bed. I just knew he had a more exciting life than ironing handkerchiefs every Saturday."

"And now?"

"I don't know. I suppose Aunt Leila was okay. She did the best she could with a child she didn't ask for. She didn't have any children of her own."

He took her hand. "She was probably happy to have you then."

"Maybe." She looked at their hands joined together. "Don't you ever feel cheated because you didn't have a chance to be an astronaut?"

"Not really. I'm not much for beating the system. I think the way I was raised made me a team player."

"Really?" She smiled. "I didn't notice that about you."

"I leave the rebellious stuff to people like you." He kissed her hand.

The moon made shadows on his face as his mouth touched the back of her hand. The whole moment made her feel unreal. He looked like some dark prince. She was walking down a moonlit street in a dream. It made the light kiss he placed on her hand tingle.

"Let's get something to eat." She snatched her hand from him. Panic pushed her through the doorway of a large pizza place.

The restaurant was brightly lit and noisy. Maggie was inside before Adam could say that he was hoping for someplace a little cozier. It was too late. He followed her past the pool table and six giant TV screens that were carrying the Falcons' football game.

"This is a great place, isn't it?" she remarked as she found a seat.

He leaned his head closer to her. "What?"

"This is a great place," she enthused again, louder. She pulled down her skirt then recalled that she didn't need to as she felt the length of material touch her calves.

"Yes," he shouted back at her.

"I'll have a Coke," she told the waiter.

"Coke for me too," Adam yelled.

"This is great," she said with a bright, fake smile.

He took her hand in his and said something. She couldn't

hear him so she bent closer until his breath tickled her ear as he spoke. "What are you afraid of?"

"What do you mean?" she demanded, drawing back from him.

He glanced around them. "You brought us in here because you're scared. I know all the signs."

"I'm not scared!"

The waiter put their drinks on the table. Adam picked them up, slid out of the booth and walked back towards the rear of the building. Maggie watched him. She'd have to follow or look stupid. She stalked after him. He put the two Cokes side-by-side on a table in a darker, quieter part of the restaurant.

He slid close to the wall on the seat. "You were saying?"

Maggie gazed at him without speaking. She moved her Coke defiantly close to his and sat down. "I'm not afraid of you, Adam."

"Really?" He sipped his drink. "Okay, if you're not afraid of me, what *are* you afraid of?"

"I'm not afraid of anything."

"I'm afraid," he admitted. "I'm afraid of getting too involved with you."

"Really?" She looked at him wide eyed, amazed at his admission. "Why?"

"It's not just you, I guess. You were right today. I'm afraid of getting too involved with anyone after what happened between Vickie and me. Mostly, I take care of Jordan and work a lot to make up for the fact that I don't have a personal life. You do the same thing."

Maggie disagreed. "My work is very demanding."

"I'm sure."

"I have thirty kids to keep off the street, bills to pay and mouths to feed. I don't have time for a personal life."

"And you *like* it that way," he countered. "Is it because your father left you? Are you afraid anyone you care about will leave you?"

"I'm the counselor," she reminded him tartly. "I'm not afraid. Just careful."

"Careful? Have you ever had a serious relationship with a man?"

"Define serious," she replied.

"Serious. Let me see. The kind where you'd like to be with that man forever. Where you'd give up the shelter or anything else to be with him. The kind where you lay in bed at night and wonder what it would be like at that moment just to have him near you."

She sipped her Coke. It was flat but she acted like it was the best she ever had. "I think we should order some pizza. What do you like on yours?"

He put his hand on top of hers. "Have you ever felt like that, Maggie?"

The closest I've ever come is with you. "I wouldn't want to feel that way."

"Ah."

"What does that mean?"

"It means *ah.*" He smiled at her.

"Adam, don't analyze me!"

"I know a kindred spirit when I see one," he insisted. "You're afraid, too. You've given yourself plenty to do so that you don't have to think about it too much. Lots of people around you like a surrogate family. But we're both fakes. Neither one of us are busier than Delta and Dan. They have a relationship."

"They were looking for one," she retaliated.

"My point exactly. They were looking for one. Both of us are too afraid to have one."

Maggie slid down in the seat. "Don't you think I've said that to myself?"

"I don't know. I can go a long time without thinking about it." He was surprised by her honesty.

"Yeah, me, too. Except when I see Delta and Dan together. Or when—"

He laughed at her. "When I came barging into your life?"

He'd been honest with her about his feelings. She could be honest, too. "Yes."

"It's funny," he admitted, "I never thought of you as anything except a thorn in my side until that morning."

"What changed?" She didn't look at him. She didn't want to see the answer in his beautiful eyes.

"I don't know. But I had this *urge*—" His finger followed a strand of her hair down to her collarbone.

Maggie shivered. "Oh those. I understand *urges*."

"But not relationships? That's the big scary demon?"

"I know it's best for me not to take anyone too seriously. I think that's what happened to my father. He was trapped for a while with my mother and me. When she died, he was finally able to escape. I don't want to live my life that way."

Adam studied her face as she spoke. "But were they happy together while she was alive?"

"My aunt said they weren't. I—I can't remember."

"And what do you do with the . . . *urges?*"

He said the words close enough to her ear that his breath brushed her sensitive neck. She was hot and cold at once, shivering on the outside but hot as lava on the inside. "I ignore them. Or I bury them in my work. My life is pretty complicated. I decided a long time ago that I was more interested in being there for the kids."

Adam sat back away from her. "You sound just like me. I wasn't expecting John to die and leave Jordan with me. I wasn't prepared for the complications of taking care of a child."

Maggie grinned. "Instant fatherhood, huh?"

"You could say that." Someone turned up the sound on the Falcon's game. The TV was blaring. Adam threw down a few bills on the table and grabbed her hand. "My condo is only a couple of blocks away. I'm brave enough to ask you to come and let me cook dinner for you. Are you brave enough to accept?"

Maggie wondered what it was about him that touched her so deeply. What made him so special to her? To say that she wanted to go with him was as much of an understatement as comparing a flea to an eagle. She *longed* to go with him.

It was against everything she ever thought was true. Against all of her principles. But she stood up and waited for him to get to his feet. "I'm brave enough to accept *and* eat that dinner, Adam. Because Jordan told me that you're a great cook. The best we ever get at the shelter is macaroni and cheese."

He laughed down at her. "You're a brave soul, Maggie Madison, because Jordan's favorite food is frozen pizza. I make great microwave meals. Still want to come?"

She picked up her Coke and tossed back the rest of the drink. "I'm up to the challenge!"

They walked out of the crowded restaurant. Maggie shivered in the freezing air.

He wrapped his arm around her. "Cold? Or scared?"

"Since I know we're having frozen food, a little of both."

He wrapped half of his warm coat around her. She snuggled close to him and he kissed her lips lightly. "I'm willing to admit that you scare me, Maggie. You make me feel stupid and angry and totally out of control. I don't know what's going to happen next or what I'm supposed to do."

She put her mouth to his and took his next words with her lips. It was supposed to be a quick, random kiss. It became something more as his warmth and scent wrapped around her. She raised her head finally and she was leaning against him, breathing hard. Her thoughts were scattered, devoid of any meaning except the need to be closer to him.

"That's what I'm talking about." He was breathing hard, too. His back was against the hard brick wall where she pushed him. Her hands were gripping his jacket lapels.

She shivered again. "I'm beginning to *feel* like a frozen pizza out here, Adam."

"Liar!" He kissed her, sliding his hands around her warm body. "You feel like I could cook a frozen pizza *without* the oven!"

"Are you refusing to take me to your condo?" She stroked her fingers through his hair and leisurely kissed the side of his mouth and his cheek. "Is this your technique? Ask a girl to dinner then make her beg for food?"

He kissed her neck by her ear. She shivered again and arched her body against his until he groaned. "No. I just want you to admit that you're not cold anymore." He traced his hand down her supple spine. "This doesn't happen between two people everyday, Maggie. I'm willing to take a chance if you are."

"This? You mean two people standing on a street corner making out? Because I'm pretty sure I've seen a lot of *this* but—"

"Maggie!"

"Oh, all right." She gave in with a deep sigh. "But can we eat first before we change the natural order of the world?"

Laughing, Adam moved away from the wall. He kept her pressed against his side, still wrapped in his coat. "Let's go!"

They walked the few blocks to Adam's condo. Maggie wasn't sure afterward what they talked about. The whole night was becoming an unbelievable fantasy for her. She knew she'd wake up at some point and find that her prince was really a frog.

"There's frozen pizza. Frozen pasta. Frozen burritos," Adam told her as he looked through his freezer.

Maggie squeezed next to him and looked into the freezer. "Do you really eat frozen food all the time?"

He looked hurt. "Do I criticize your macaroni and cheese?"

"No." She opened the refrigerator door. "But you've got some real food here. I think we could make something better than that."

Together, they hauled out some plain rice left over from Chinese take-out. Maggie found some frozen peppers and onions that she added to the pan.

Adam went in search of a bottle of wine. "What kind of music do you like?"

She found some garlic and chopped it into tiny bits. "I like the old stuff, mainly classic rock."

He put on a CD. "How about Vivaldi?"

Maggie shrugged and tossed the sizzling rice and vegetables with some soy sauce. "I don't know who that is but it sounds interesting. You like classical music, I'm not surprised."

With Vivaldi coming through the speakers, Adam came back to the kitchen and searched for a corkscrew. "It goes with the gray suits I guess."

Before he could open the bottle of wine, Maggie turned and hugged him. "I'm sorry. I didn't mean to hurt your feelings. You look good in your gray suits."

He let go of the wine bottle and took her in his arms. "Jordan said that I might be cool for an old man."

She smiled and touched the side of his face. "I guess you could be. You're pretty good looking for an old man. If you wear jeans and tennis shoes enough, it might make you a little less ogrely."

He kissed her lightly. "I *feel* less ogrely around you."

"I have that effect on people. Just last month, I changed a troll into a respected member of the community."

"What about you, Maggie?" He searched her face earnestly. "What will close association with an ogre do to you?"

"I guess we'll find out," Maggie told him. "It already made my skirt longer."

Adam laughed. "What made you keep coming back to my office? No one else could be that crazy."

She kissed his forehead and the side of his mouth. "I'm persistent and goal-oriented. Besides, you were so handsome in a dark, threatening way. I just knew you needed rescuing from that evil fortress."

"I'm so glad you rescued me." He kissed her again.

Maggie wound her arms around his neck. For once, she could block out the fear that usually paralyzed her when she knew she might be facing a relationship with a man.

She forgot everything when he kissed her. Only the smell of scorching rice forced them apart.

"I guess that means we should eat." Adam knew he had a large, dopey smile on his face. He didn't care. Holding Maggie was as exciting and challenging as the idea of being an astronaut ever was to him.

It was late when they finally left Adam's condo. They walked down the sidewalk together, past the nightclubs and expensive trendy restaurants. A group of teenagers swarmed out of a local hangout, almost knocking them down as they tore down the sidewalk.

"Are you okay?" Adam asked her.

"I'm fine." She laughed. "It's a lot like being at the shelter in the morning!"

"That's why you wear the boots all the time," he suggested. "To keep yourself firmly anchored down."

"Exactly! There's a big difference between one teenager and twenty-five."

He shook his head. "I know! I've never heard so much bickering."

"Didn't you and your brother ever argue?"

"My parents would've stepped in before it got too bad. Not that there were times when things got out of hand. Being an only child, I'm surprised you handle it as well as you do."

"Maybe it's *because* I'm an only child," she answered. "I missed all of that noise and bickering. It was just Aunt Leila and me. Sometimes, I prayed for something to happen just to liven things up a little."

"Have you ever thought about having your own children to make up for it?" He held her close and smiled down into her face. "The children you take in off the street are never going to be the same as your own."

"As much as I love the kids at the shelter, I wouldn't want to have any of my own," she declared. "I've thought about it a lot. It's not something I need to do. There are already too many children out there who don't have parents who want them."

Adam frowned. "Have you thought about adopting?"

"I have a house with twenty-five to thirty kids a night. And if your plan goes well, there'll be more than that. Why would I need any of my own?"

"Having Jordan has been a big thing in my life," he admitted. "I never thought about being a father until John died. I was sorry when Vickie and I broke up. She wanted children too."

Maggie had that conversation before with friends of hers who were safely settled down into mortgages and babies. There was always an underlying feeling that something was wrong with her if she didn't want her own children. She was quick on the defense. "I think it's fine, if that's the life you choose. I just don't feel the need to have my own biological children."

She looked into his dark face as they passed a red neon sign that spelled out *EAT.* Would it matter to him? Possibly. But this was a matter that had been decided in her mind a long time ago. It was affected by her feelings about her own childhood. It also made sense to her not to bring another child into an overcrowded world.

"I'm sorry." He touched a finger to her lips.

"What? What for?" She gulped and jumped to conclusions. He couldn't cope. Any relationship they might have had was over before it began. Maybe it was better that way.

"For causing that frown. You don't have to defend yourself to me, Maggie. When Vickie and I were dating, her mother ragged on us all the time about having a baby. It wasn't much fun."

Maggie reconsidered. Maybe she was wrong. Maybe he was okay with her decision. This was too much like being on a roller coaster. "It's okay. People expect me to be a certain way because of what I do. I guess I'm different than I'm supposed to be."

Adam kissed her. "I like you the way you are."

"When I'm agreeing with you," she answered brightly, glad that he was willing to drop the subject.

"Of course. I'm never right with Jordan. I have to be right sometimes."

"That might be difficult," she said with a smile, "since I'm always right."

"Always?" Adam stopped abruptly outside a small coffee house. The loud, smooth sound of jazz spilled out into the street and surrounded them. He glanced at the poster on the door. "What are the chances?"

Maggie looked where he was pointing. It was a poster for a band called The Great Little Jazz Band. It featured Brewster Madison with his song *Maggie Girl.* Fear swamped her. She tugged on his sleeve. "We should go."

"Aren't you curious?"

"Not at all. Can we go now?"

"Let's go inside for a few minutes, Maggie." He pulled her along with him.

Half swallowed by his coat, his arm tightly around her, she had no choice. She was swept along with him. Short of creating a scene at the entrance to the coffee shop, there was no way to pull away from him. "Adam, *please!*"

Adam was so curious about how this man could have Maggie's last name and a song with her name in it, he didn't notice her hesitation. He stepped into the dark room that was redolent with the aroma of coffee. Smoke hung heavily. It was almost impossible to see where he was going. He managed to find a vacant table at the back. The sax was moaning. The man who sat at the microphone was singing with his eyes closed, deeply engrossed in his music. "This is great, huh?"

"I hate this music," she whispered, refusing to look at the stage. "Can we go now?"

"What's wrong, Maggie?"

"Care to order?" the waiter asked as Maggie disentangled herself from Adam's coat.

"Nothing for me," she told him tersely.

"We have some fantastic dark roast Kenyan. The flavor of the day is cinnamon hazelnut."

"We'll both have espresso," Adam ordered as he sat down beside Maggie. "Don't you like espresso?"

"That's fine. I don't care!" She put her hands up to her face. She didn't want to tell him what was wrong.

"You don't have to drink it."

"Can we just leave, please?"

Adam was trying to be more spontaneous and exciting. Instead he felt embarrassed and stupid. *You can't change a tiger's stripes.* Didn't his father tell him that? He wasn't sure what it meant . . . until that moment. Spontaneous and exciting just wasn't his thing. Hadn't Vickie made that very clear? He got to his feet. "Okay. Let's go."

The lights came up while the audience was applauding. The band was taking a break. Maggie tugged at his hand. "Sit down. Sit down! We can't go *now!*"

He took his seat, totally confused. "Maggie, what's the problem?"

"He might see us!"

"Who?" Adam looked around the room.

"Brewster Madison."

Lightning struck Adam. *My father was a musician.* Madison. Maggie. "Brewster? Your *father?"*

"Yes!" Maggie ducked her head down close to the table and tried to hide behind Adam.

"I had no idea." He glanced up at the stage. "I didn't think. I'm sorry."

"It's okay." She was breathing rapidly, glancing around the room like she was a criminal on the run. "We can wait until the lights go down again and then sneak out."

Adam lowered his head to the level of hers. "Don't you even want to see him?"

"I haven't seen him or spoken to him since he left me with my aunt. I didn't realize this was the place he was playing. I wouldn't have come anywhere near it."

"So you knew he was in Atlanta?"

She nodded.

"Maggie, he's your father."

"Biologically," she agreed angrily. "But he wasn't there when I needed him. I don't want to sit around having coffee with him and pretending it's all right because he's decided he wants to see me."

Adam considered her words. "You've purposely avoided him all these years but he wants to see you?"

"Every time he comes to town," she explained. "He writes to me or calls me. We go through this."

"I don't understand."

"It doesn't matter," she hissed, watching the stage for the return of the band. She'd never come this close to seeing her father.

"Evening," a friendly voice greeted them.

Maggie picked up the large sandwich menu and hid behind it.

"I hope you're enjoying the show."

"We are." Adam glanced hesitantly at Maggie. "We just got here. It's been great so far."

"I don't recognize you. I'm Brewster Madison." He extended his hand to Adam. "Usually we attract the same group of fans every time we're in town. In fact, I'm thinking about buying this place as our permanent home."

Adam shook his hand. He tried to see something of Maggie in the other man's face. But the lighting was bad and Brewster Madison looked nothing like his daughter. "That sounds like a good move."

"After the break, I'm gonna be singing our one and only single that ever made it to the charts. It topped out at a hundred. But *Maggie Girl* is still my favorite song."

"I guess that's better than not making it to the charts at all!"

"Exactly, my friend—?"

"Adam Fuentes."

"Nice to meet you, Adam. Who's your shy friend behind the menu?"

"She's not feeling well," Adam lied smoothly. "We're probably going to call it a night."

"Oh. Too bad. Come back and tell the guy at the door I said you could get a free coffee since she got sick. Have a better night."

"You, too." Adam took a deep breath when they were alone again. "He's gone."

"I know." Maggie shuddered.

"I can't believe you haven't even seen your father in all these years. I thought he was dead the way you talked about him."

"What difference does it make?" she demanded. "Does being an adult make me all-forgiving?"

"Maggie, you give other people second and third chances all the time. I've heard you. Doesn't he deserve the same?"

"This isn't something we can discuss," she told him bluntly. "You don't understand."

"But Maggie—"

The lights went down low again and the music started. Maggie got to her feet and tossed the menu on the table. "I'm out of here."

Adam paid the bill and grabbed his coat. It took him a few minutes to catch up with her on the street. "Hey, wait a minute!"

"I'm going back to the shelter."

What about me? He wanted to ask but the words wouldn't come out. He'd used up his store of spontaneity and excitement for a year or two that evening. It didn't serve him well. "I'm sorry. I didn't know your father would be there."

She was marching down the sidewalk with all the impact of an army. When she heard his apology, she took a deep breath and slowed down. "I'm sorry, Adam. I didn't mean to ruin the evening."

"You didn't ruin it. I guess it just got cut short a little."

"I knew my father was in town. I always know. I've never run into him before." She looked away from him. "I hope it never happens again."

Adam still didn't understand her reasoning. "He's your

father, Maggie. No matter what he did wrong all those years ago."

She turned on him in an instant. "Your father didn't desert you! You don't know what it's like to lose both of your parents when you're a child."

"That's true. But I'm Jordan's uncle. Even though I don't know what it's like, I try my best to be there for her. I hope she'll be able to forgive me if I'm not perfect."

Maggie started walking again. "No one's perfect. But at least we all try to do our best. *He* didn't even try."

"Are you sure?" Adam continued even though he could see she didn't like it.

"Am I sure he didn't try?" She pushed her hair back from her face. "I got a letter from him for the first time after Aunt Leila died. I was 20 years old. I wouldn't call that trying, Adam."

"All I'm saying is that—"

"I don't want to talk about it!"

Her stubborn refusal to talk about it made him angry. "It's all right to discuss my problems, but not yours?"

"This isn't a problem for me. In fact, I never even think about him once I throw his letter in the trash."

"Maggie, stand still a minute." He grabbed her arm.

She shook him off. "Go away, Adam."

He stopped her forward movement again. "I won't go away because you don't want to see your father. Talk to me."

Maggie faced him with fury freezing her face. "Don't you see? He's what shaped my whole life. I spent the first ten years of my life wondering what was wrong with me. Why he didn't want me. Then I spent a few years trying to get in touch with him. Finally I figured it out. It wasn't me. It was *him*. He was wrong. He let me down. He didn't want to share my life. He chose not to do that when I was a child. I've chosen not to share my life with him as an adult."

"Does that make you right?" he whispered, pulling her close to him.

"No. It makes me a survivor. I survived *despite* him. He can survive without me."

Adam held her without saying another word. There was nothing he could say.

She pulled away from him after a few minutes and scrubbed her eyes with her sleeves. "I'm sorry. I didn't mean to get so worked up about it."

"It's okay." He smiled at her.

"Now my face is all blotchy. I look like an ad for cosmetic surgery."

Adam hugged her again and looked down into her tear stained face. "You look beautiful to me."

Maggie searched for something she didn't ever expect to find in a man's eyes. *Understanding and acceptance.* "Why are you here, Adam? Why aren't you in your office working tonight?"

"Because you needed me to be here." He kissed the tip of her nose then kissed each teary eye. "And because you kept pestering me to be in your life."

She laughed. "You're right. I asked for it. And here you are."

"Here I am. Wet and exhausted from trying to keep up with you. What do you say to some real coffee at the shelter? I hear the coffee there will make your hair stand on end."

Maggie sniffed and smiled. "Well, that's a step down from espresso but I guess it will do."

"We have real artificial creamer to go in it," he enticed her as they started to walk together again.

"In that case, count me in." Shc laughed. "You really know how to sweet talk a girl."

He shrugged his broad shoulders. "I learned it all from a persistent solicitor."

She stopped at the door before they went into the house. It was very quiet on the sidewalk. The moon was still spreading a silver sheen on the night. "Thanks, Adam."

"My pleasure."

"You're a very good man."

He rolled his eyes. "The kiss of death. Next thing you know, you'll be telling me that you only want to be friends."

"Not every woman is Vickie." She grabbed his coat and drew him to her.

Chapter Ten

"Someone might consider goodness to be an excellent trait." She kissed his chin. "Even a sexy trait."

"Maybe." He traced the edge of her cold ear with his warm finger. "We should go inside. You're freezing."

"In a minute." She brought his face down close to hers. She kissed him gently on the mouth. He tasted like peppermint and coffee and smelled like the clear night air.

He leaned back against his car and brought her closer still. "I have a hard time keeping up with you, Maggie."

She sighed and nuzzled his throat before she kissed him again. "I'm not usually so scattered. And if we don't count arguing about my father, I think it's been a pretty good night. My dates tend to be disasters."

Adam whispered, "So are mine."

"Is this too crazy for you?"

He smiled. "It's a lot like being sucked up into a tornado. It's crazy. But it's a nice kind of crazy."

She slipped her arm through his and snuggled close to him. "Maybe we should go inside and have that coffee you were talking about."

"Maggie?" Delta's voice rang out in the quiet night. "Come quick!"

"I'm right here." Maggie sighed and moved away from Adam. "What's wrong? Is there a problem with the toilet again?"

Delta peered through the darkness. "Is that Adam out there with you?"

"Yes," Maggie answered. "And I don't want to hear any jokes about it either."

"This is serious, honey. Get Adam in here, too. Jordan's run away again. Robbie and Kevin went with her.

Maggie scrambled to reach the door.

Adam did the same. "Why would Jordan run away now?"

"One thing I've learned," Maggie held the door for him, "is that the things kids do don't always make sense to adults. I think they make sense to them at the time but not to anyone else."

"Did Delta say she'd gone off with *two* boys?"

"I don't know. Let's get the whole story before we jump to conclusions." Maggie tried to keep him calm.

"I can't win with that girl," Adam lamented. "Maybe Leslie's family would have better luck with her."

"Don't start talking like that yet. We'll find her. The two boys are probably Kevin and Robbie. The boys who were fighting when we came upstairs last week? They've been fighting over Jordan. I thought they reached some kind of understanding."

He couldn't believe it. "You could've told me."

She reached up and brushed back a stray lock of his hair away from his forehead. "I thought it was taken care of. I didn't think it was something to worry about."

"Nothing seems to be that way with Jordan right now."

"Don't be too tough on her," Maggie advised. "She's going through a hard time."

"One that could be made better if I wasn't so stubborn about keeping her with me?"

Maggie looked into his face. "No. I don't believe that. And I haven't told her that either. If you give her up now, you'll both be sorry. And she'll be running away from her mother's family. When you listen to her, she always talks about you not spending enough time with her. Doesn't that tell you something?"

Adam hung his jacket up by the floor. "Yeah. It tells me that she's doing this to irritate me enough to let her go. She wants to go to Canada."

She realized that he was too emotional right now to reason with him. "Never mind. Come on. Let's find her."

Adam wanted to call the police right away. Maggie and Delta wanted to be sure the girl was gone.

"Once the police are involved, there's no going back for Kevin or Robbie," Delta told him. "They'll be in Juvvie."

"Maybe that would be for the best," Adam replied. "Excuse me if I'm not feeling very benevolent about them right now. They ran off with my niece."

Delta glanced at Maggie.

"Let's be sure that's what happened before we call in the Marines," Maggie suggested. "You should check out your condo. Maybe Jordan got tired of sleeping on the cot and just went back home. There's no note. We're just guessing at what happened right now."

"Okay," Adam agreed reluctantly. "I'll call if I see them. Here's my cell phone number. Call me if they show up."

Maggie and Delta watched him leave. As soon as the Mercedes was out of the driveway, Maggie pulled on her coat and gloves. "I'm going out after them."

"Was sending him on a spook hunt a good idea?" Delta questioned. "Won't he be even angrier when he doesn't find her there?"

"Maybe. On the other hand, it will give him a few minutes to calm down before he sees her. If he's too upset, it'll only make things worse."

"You know best. And it looked to me like you know him pretty well."

"Nothing happened." Maggie opened the door. "I'm not getting into that right now."

"Oooh! I think you were already into that, honey!"

Maggie ignored her. "I'll let you know if I see them or hear anything."

"And there you were giving me and Dan those nasty

looks and we were just in the *family* room! Not right out there in public."

"Goodbye!" Maggie left the house, refusing to acknowledge Delta's jokes about her and Adam.

She tucked her head down against the icy wind that blew along the street. Why were there so many more problems in the winter? Why didn't more kids run away in the summer when it was warm? It was a lot warmer and a lot more fun sharing Adam's coat.

That thought spewed up an entire volcano of other thoughts. *What am I thinking?* More to the point, when did she *stop* thinking? She was standing outside like a teenager, making out against Adam's car. He was right to think about how crazy it was.

Adam had a devastating effect on her. In only a week, she'd changed her mind about the possibility of a long-term relationship. She saw her father for the first time since she was a child. Even worse, being married to Adam was starting to sound pretty good. Not that he mentioned anything about love or commitment. And that was a whole other level of thought. Her life was a mess.

She put her hands into her pockets when she reached the street and ran right into Adam. "What are you doing here? I thought you were going back to the condo?"

He held up his cell phone. "I set the alarm at the condo before I left. All I had to do was call the security company. Jordan hasn't been there. But you knew that, didn't you?"

Maggie saw the Mercedes parked at the curb. "You waited down here so I wouldn't know you didn't go back there?"

"Until I saw what you were going to do." He fell in step beside her. "Where are we going?"

"*We're* not going anywhere," she said flatly. "*I'm* going to see if I can find Kevin and Robbie. Maybe Jordan is with them."

"Stop playing with me, Maggie," he answered irritably. "We both know Jordan is with them. You sent me on a wild goose chase."

"I *think* Jordan is with Robbie and Kevin. I won't know for sure until we find them. All the more reason for you to stay at the shelter and let me take care of this part."

"That doesn't make any sense."

"Really?" Maggie looked at him. "We both know that when you and Jordan see each other, the fur's going to fly. You can be calm and mature about this and help her, or you can be as angry as you are right now and make it worse."

"That works for me." He ran across the street.

She waited for a car to pass before she followed him. "You're impossible."

"You've told me that before."

"I can't stop you from going?"

"No."

"Fine." She huddled in her coat and walked faster. "Then you'll just have to keep up."

Long moments passed as they walked up the usually busy street in the darkness. The night had turned cold enough to make the wind sting their noses and ears. Maggie felt like crying when she thought about where they were before this happened. Looking back on it, she guessed it was insanity that made her kiss him. *Insanity and a healthy libido!* She glanced at Adam quickly, wondering if he was thinking about it, too.

"Sorry if I'm walking too fast for you." She couldn't stand the silence between them any longer.

"Not for me. Those legs aren't that long."

Maggie looked away self-consciously. Her heart was beating faster than it should be because of the walk. "What about Jordan?"

"Maggie, I'm here," Adam said grimly. "I'm not leaving until we find her. Just live with it."

"That's not what I mean. I mean have you thought about what you'll say to Jordan when we find her." Maggie was beginning to wonder what it was about him that she found so attractive just a short while before.

"I don't know. What am I supposed to say? You tell me

she's trying to get my attention. I've all but given up working for the past week while we've been going through this. What else can I do?"

She scuffed her boot on the sidewalk. "It's a lifestyle change. She knows this is a different time and what you've given up to do this. But what's going to change when you get back home?"

"What you're asking is impossible!" Adam's voice was irritated. "I can't run my business by only working two hours a day!"

She argued, "What about normal working hours? Jordan's in school every day."

"It's not that simple."

"No. I suppose it's not."

Adam knew what she was thinking. "This isn't the same thing as your father leaving you, Maggie. I'm fighting to keep Jordan with me. But I can't give up my business or we'll both be spending quality time together on the street."

She stopped walking and faced him. "You told me that we're alike. I think you're right. I'm not looking for a serious relationship with anyone. I spend a lot of time at my job. I realize that you're trying to get over Vickie by working too much. But you've already got Jordan in your life. Aren't you looking for a serious relationship with her?"

Adam didn't speak for a long time. The wind rushed past, making them both shiver. "Maybe you're right. I don't know. I've tried to work through this thing that happened with Vickie. I've tried not to let it affect my life with Jordan. But I'm only human, Maggie. I can only do the best I can."

She grabbed his arms and shook him a little. "If you're really doing that, there won't be a problem. But working ninety hours a week isn't doing the best you can do!"

Adam followed her as she stalked off again. "What about you?"

"What about me?" she yelled back. "I don't have a single, permanent child to devote time to. My kids and I have temporary relationships."

"And you like it that way," he accused. "You wouldn't even speak to your father tonight!"

"That's not the same thing."

"Only because you can give advice but not take it!"

"Oh?" she queried. "Is this from a parental perspective?"

"Yes I don't know what your father went through to leave you with your aunt. But if he wants to see you now, maybe it was the best he could do. Maybe he was afraid he couldn't raise you alone. That thought strikes me every three and a half minutes of every day! And I'm not even Jordan's real father."

"Let's leave my personal life out of this," she recommended. "This is about you and Jordan."

"No, this is about relationships and how to protect yourself from having one."

She ignored him. "There's the camp where we found Robbie. I think they've probably come back here. I think he still has family here."

"And you're going to change the subject."

"Adam, we have to focus here."

"Okay," he agreed, switching gears to focus on their problem. "So you think Jordan's in there with Robbie?"

"It's a place he knows well enough to feel safe. I can't figure why he and Kevin would leave but they probably don't know that either." She looked up at him with a sigh. "I don't want to attract any extra attention. This can be a dangerous place. Are you sure you won't go back?"

His only reply was a shuttered look to his eyes.

"I can't make you go home," she looked straight ahead into the night, "but please, try to hold on to what you have to say until we get out of here."

"I'll do the best I can."

They stood together for a few minutes, not saying anything.

"You can tell it's a cold night." Maggie focused on something she could handle. "Lots of fires."

"Maybe you should let me look for them." The large

number of people outside the old brick building made Adam nervous. "You said yourself it could be dangerous."

"If I backed off every time I was scared, I couldn't do my job."

"You're the most stubborn woman I've ever known."

"We already covered that issue."

"Maggie?"

"Adam." She stopped and looked up at him. There was a dark shadow on his jaw. His expressive mouth was a grim line in his lean face. "I'll be fine. I do this all the time. People know me here. Maybe you should go back."

"I'm not leaving you here alone."

"Fine."

"Fine."

They walked side by side to where an old shell of a building created shelter against the frozen night air. Fires in rusted barrels provided a little warmth while chair legs and parts of old pallets served as the wood supply. The moonlit night was full of people in pain. They groaned and sighed like the wind. They gathered together, despite the danger that came with being in a group. A small pocket of outcast humanity in the dark night.

Maggie walked the rounds twice, hoping for a glimpse of one of the kids. She knew it could be all night or several nights before she might spot them. She also knew that they could have left the city. If so, they might never find them. She didn't want to say that to Adam. She didn't want to believe that Jordan would be that stupid either. But she knew it could happen.

"What if she's not here?" Adam asked as they finished walking by all of the barrels that blazed orange light up at the sky.

"We wait." Maggie plopped down on a piece of broken cement not too close to the fires. "It might take some time."

He sat beside her. He looked out at the remnants of people who could have been his uncle or his brothers. The size of the problem hit him. "What you do for them is like a drop in the bucket, isn't it?"

"Yes." She nodded and rubbed her hands together for warmth. "But every drop I save and help to get off the street is one less drop out here. I may only be able to handle thirty kids at a time but they would *all* be here right now if I couldn't. The kids are the most likely to change. If I can give them something to work for, something to hope for, I can prevent them from being adults in shelters."

"I admire your passion and commitment to them."

"Thanks. It would be hard *not* to be passionate and committed to them after everything I've seen."

"They feel the same about you, you know," Adam told her. "I've heard the kids talking about you at the shelter. They really look up to you. Whatever caused those two boys to leave with Jordan has to be something serious."

She laughed. "You mean they're both in love with the same girl and neither one wants to let the other gain any ground?"

"You're talking about my niece, Maggie!"

"I'm talking about a reason powerful enough to make them both lose everything. Robbie and Kevin have been out here. They know they'll go to Juvvie or end up out here again after this. Sex can be a powerful motivator." *Don't I know it!*

"They're just kids."

"What were you thinking about when you were thirteen, Adam? Besides working with your father and being an astronaut. What else consumed you?"

Even in the dim, smoky light, it was easy to see the awareness on his face as he considered her question.

"And that's what *they're* thinking too!"

"Jordan's innocent," Adam swore after realizing what the boys were thinking. What he'd been thinking about almost nonstop at their age.

"She might be innocent but Mother Nature provides everything she needs to know without experience. She probably had those two fighting to see who was going to run away with her."

He didn't disagree this time. There were too many things

he hadn't thought about in a long time. Wanting to be an astronaut and his thirteen-year-old feelings about girls among them. "I'm sorry I didn't see that before."

"I'm glad you can see it now."

"Meaning I was too pig-headed to see it before?"

"Meaning that some people never see it and—"

Adam put his finger to her lips. "We're doing it again."

"It?" she said around his hand.

"We have a tendency to argue or—"

She shivered. "Never mind."

He got up and stamped his feet, rubbing his hands together for warmth. "Isn't there something else we can do besides wait here and hope to see them? Maybe we should call the police."

"Sometimes, people have to know you out here." She nodded towards the person who was approaching them. "They don't tell the police anything. But they might tell me."

The woman walked right up to them. She was wearing two coats and shabby gloves. "You're the lady from the shelter?"

She was wearing too many layers of clothes to be able to tell any shape or form, but Maggie thought she recognized her voice. "I'm from The Small Miracles Shelter."

"I know. You're Maggie Madison. You helped my boy, Josh, a while back. He's in the Army now. He's a good boy."

"Thanks for telling me. I'm glad he made it."

"We heard Robbie Black was staying at your place. I saw him tonight with another boy and a girl. They're spending the night up at the old switch house by the tracks. Know where I mean?"

"Yes." Maggie got up and dusted off her bottom. "Thanks for your help."

"You do a good job with the kids. Take care."

Adam waited to speak until the woman left. "How far is it?"

"Not far."

"What are we waiting for?"

Maggie was staring past him, not moving. Adam turned to look. Jordan was with Kevin and Robbie. They were escorted by two police officers. As they got closer, he realized that one of them was Dan.

Dan left his partner behind with the kids. "Looking for someone?"

Maggie nodded. "There was something missing at the shelter. Where'd you find them?"

"There was a drug bust up at the old switch house. I knew they belonged to you. I thought they probably weren't involved with the drugs. When I heard you were out here, I brought them along with me."

"Are you going to arrest them?" Adam didn't look at his niece.

"Nope. Not this time anyway. If I catch any of them in a situation like this again, there won't be any stopping it."

"Thanks, Dan." Adam shook his hand.

"What about these two?" Dan asked, with a nod at the two boys.

Maggie steeled herself. She stared at Robbie and Kevin. "They'll have to go to Juvvie."

"Ms. Madison!" Kevin yelled. "Give us another chance."

"You've had your chances. And you know the rule about being out after curfew. There's nothing else I can do for you right now. Too many other kids would like to have your beds and obey the rules."

"Ms. Madison?" Robbie implored her with his words and eyes. "Not Juvvie!"

"I'm sorry, Robbie."

"Okay." Dan spoke to the other officer and told him to take the two boys away. He looked at Maggie. "Could I have a minute with you?"

Maggie's shoulders slumped as she watched them being led away. "Sure."

Adam excused himself. "I need to talk to Jordan."

Dan shoved his hands in his pockets. "Delta broke up with me tonight."

"Oh, Dan, I'm so sorry. You two seemed so good together."

"I thought so." He shrugged. "Listen, Maggie, I hate to ask, but would you talk to her? Try to help me understand what went wrong?"

She put her hand on his arm. "I'll talk to her. No promises. But I'll ask."

"Thanks. That's all I'm asking for."

Maggie took a deep breath that felt like ice in her lungs. Adam and Jordan were standing apart like Sumo wrestlers, glaring at each other.

"Are you all right?" Adam finally asked his niece. "Why did you leave?"

"I'm fine, Uncle Adam." Jordan hugged her arms tightly to her chest. "I don't know why I left."

Adam struggled for words. He was furious. He wanted to take her home and lock her in her room for a week before he spoke to her. And he was terrified. He thought being out there with the homeless was bad. She'd been involved in a drug bust!

"This is my fault," Jordan told Maggie. "I got them to go with me. Don't punish them."

Adam couldn't believe she was trying to help the boys. "Jordan, you've caused enough trouble."

"Maybe you should just let me go to Canada then, huh, Uncle Adam?" She defied him. "Maybe mom's family won't think I'm too much trouble!"

"We're going back to our place now!"

"Fine! But I won't be happy there. I'll keep running away!"

He stared at her angrily. "Then maybe you're right. Maybe you should go to Canada if you're so unhappy with me."

"Uncle Adam!"

"Since that's what you want so much and you're willing to risk your life to make your point, how can I say no?"

"You never listen to me!"

"Adam," Maggie cautioned quietly.

"Let's go." He ushered his niece before him, ignoring Maggie.

Maggie walked silently back to the shelter with them. She didn't know anything to say that wouldn't make it worse. When they got there, Jordan told her uncle that she needed some things from her makeshift bedroom in the shelter. He replied curtly that he would pick her things up later. He closed her car door and got behind the wheel. He didn't say a word to Maggie.

"What happened?" Delta asked when she saw Maggie.

"We found them." Maggie collapsed at one of the tables. "They were almost involved in a drug bust. If Dan wouldn't have been there, it would've been bad."

"You sent Kevin and Robbie to Juvvie, didn't you?"

"Did I have a choice?"

"No." Delta's voice was despondent.

They sat together for a long time, not moving or talking. Finally, Delta sighed. "So what about you and The Ogre?

"I don't know. It was just . . . crazy."

"Isn't it always?"

"This was crazier than most things. What about you and Dan?"

"It isn't going to work, Maggie. Every time I talk to him, every time I kiss him, I think about Matt. I'm not ready yet, I guess."

Maggie hugged her. "Dan's a good guy."

"I know. I can't do it yet. I can't let go of Matt." Delta got to her feet. "I'm going back to bed. I'll see you in the *real* morning."

Maggie couldn't go to sleep. She curled up in the chair by the front window in the darkness. She rested her head against the cold windowpane and let her thoughts fall randomly.

She knew from the first kiss that Adam was a mistake. He was stable and serious. If he got involved with anyone, he'd be looking for a relationship. That's what was killing him about Jordan. He wanted a relationship with the girl. He just didn't know how to have one.

Adam wasn't the kind of man who'd be happy having a good time together. He wanted something permanent. He was recovering from a bad relationship with Vickie. But it would only be a matter of time before he was looking for someone to take her place.

Maggie knew she wasn't the woman to give him what he wanted. Even though she'd started to want it too. She purposely never had a serious relationship with a man. She wasn't sure she knew how.

She wished she could've helped Jordan more. Jordan wasn't one of her street kids but she had strong feelings about what she was going through. Adam was stubbornly refusing to see what he needed to do if he wanted to keep his niece. Like her father, it was easier to give Jordan up than change his lifestyle.

The next morning, Maggie and Delta went through the motions of doing what they normally did at the shelter. They were both depressed about Kevin and Robbie. They didn't talk much. Both of them took the losses personally.

Dan came about lunchtime to tell them that the boys had left the detention center sometime during the night. "Knew they would."

"They'd rather face the streets." Maggie wasn't surprised by his announcement.

"It was the only decision you could make," he assured her.

"It doesn't make it any easier," Delta said. "I just want to hold both those boys in my arms and make it right for them."

Dan shrugged awkwardly. "You could probably find them and take them back."

"We couldn't keep the rest of the kids here under control if we let those two do whatever they want," Maggie answered. "I wish it could be different."

"Adam left with Jordan, too?"

Maggie and Delta nodded but didn't speak.

He sat beside them at the table in the kitchen. "You two

need some cheering up. How about lunch at the pita stand? My treat!"

"You go," Maggie said to Delta. "I'll stay here."

"I don't think so."

"It's okay. Just go."

"I'd rather not." Delta glared at Maggie. "Thanks anyway, Dan."

Dan looked at Maggie but all she could do was shrug her shoulders. She didn't have the answers any of them were looking for.

Delta went upstairs when Dan was gone. Maggie decided that she was going to have to do *something*. She couldn't sit at the table all day feeling sorry for herself. There was the matter of cleaning up her office. It might be a good way to purge Adam from her brain. He was there too much for her to ignore him and go on.

She poked through everything that Adam had straightened out and reorganized. No more piles of bills in shoeboxes. No more checks that they couldn't find. There were new cards in the Rolodex with names and donations. When did he find time to sleep after everything he'd done with their records?

Maggie sat down behind the big desk and turned on the computer. It felt different now. Like it wasn't hers anymore. She picked up a red and gray tie she found on a chair. It was Adam's tie. He must have dropped it. She pressed it to her face. It smelled like him. The room smelled like him, felt like him. Until it changed, she was going to question her life every time she came into her office. She closed her eyes and sat with the tie on her face while the computer was booting up.

"Maggie?"

Embarrassed, she tossed the tie to the side. "Adam?"

"What was that?"

"Ice pack. I was just using an ice pack. I have a headache."

"Oh. Sorry. I wanted to do a few things on the fundraiser this morning while I was waiting for a call. I thought I could clean up in here and take our stuff out, too. Will I be in the way?"

"No." *At this rate, the office will never be mine again.*

Adam came further into the room. "Was there something you were looking for? Maybe I can help."

"I was, uh, just checking our books. You've done such a good job with them. I was admiring them."

"Thanks. It was my pleasure. If you'd like me to, I can show you the spread sheet."

"Spread sheet?"

"Move over." He pulled a chair beside hers. "Let me show you. You should be able to access it for yourself. Then you can print it out and take it to your new accountant."

"Thanks." They were like two strangers again. *Two strangers who were kissing in the driveway just the night before!*

Chapter Eleven

He reached across her, typing in the commands while the computer did its job. She was beginning to feel very warm. Emotions that had nothing to do with accounting flooded through her. It was confusing when he touched her. When he was near her, nothing else mattered.

Adam glanced at Maggie. Was she feeling any of the electricity that was charging through him just being near her? He tried to focus on the spreadsheet he was bringing up. The woman beside him smelled like herbs and flowers. He wanted to take her in his arms and—"Here's the spreadsheet." He was grateful to see it.

"Great."

"In the green is the money as it's brought in and in the red is the money you're putting out. There's been a lot of red this month because . . ." He paused and looked at her. She was staring at him with rapt attention but her eyes were on his mouth. Distinctly. *Intently.* ". . . because of the repairs to the house." *Stay focused.*

"Uh, yeah." Maggie wished she could lean just a little closer to him.

"Maggie, I can't . . ."

"Can't?" She took a deep breath and closed her eyes. They were just inches apart. *How hard would it be to—?*

". . . can't find all the information I'm looking for." The computer screen went back to the screensaver. He sat back in his chair, panting as if he'd run a race. *She was driving him crazy.*

"Oh." Maggie was disappointed.

"I want to help you with this, I just don't know if I can."

"I understand."

"No, I don't think you do."

Maggie watched him stand up and thought that he was leaving. She wasn't prepared for him to lean over her. He slowly pushed her back in the office chair until she was almost lying flat, looking up into his face.

"Let me explain."

He kissed her. It was unlike any kiss she'd ever had before in her life. It was a kiss of passion. Of frustration and seduction. Every pore in her body exploded with it. Every hair on her body twitched in anticipation of more. It wasn't like just wanting to go out for pizza on Saturday night. This was like not having chocolate for a year and someone holding it just out of reach. This was tantalizing. It whispered into her senses until all she could feel was how much she needed him.

She whimpered in the back of her throat and slid her arms around him. In all of her life she'd never wanted anyone or anything as much as she wanted him at that moment. It was frightening and exhilarating. She knew he wanted her that much, too.

But when she reached her arms up to bring him closer, he moved away. She opened her eyes. Her lips stayed parted to protest.

Adam was shaking. He sat down again in the chair beside her. He tried to show her how much he wanted her, how much she meant to him. He only made it worse for himself. He didn't think it was possible. "Do you understand now?"

She nodded, unable to form coherent speech.

"I want more than just a one-night stand with you, Maggie. As nice as that might be." He traced her jaw line with his finger.

"You're so different than I thought you'd be," she mused, comfortable against his chest.

"But not different enough to spend time with me if you're not helping Jordan?"

"I didn't say that, Adam."

"I know you're scared to try to have a relationship."

"I'm not scared," Maggie said defensively.

"I know you're afraid of being hurt."

"I don't know what I am right now. I've always been so careful not to get involved. You're different. I admit that. But I don't know if *I've* really changed. What if it doesn't work out? I don't want to hurt you."

He took a deep breath. "You worry an awful lot about relationships for someone who doesn't want one."

"You work too hard at trying to change my mind!" she retaliated. "Didn't your breakup with Vickie teach you anything?"

Maggie knew that she hurt him. His eyes went dark and his mouth tightened. She wished she could call back the words but it was too late.

"You're a coward, Maggie. You're willing to risk your life out there on the street but you aren't brave enough to consider any kind of long-term relationship. Not with your father. Or me."

"I knew it would come down to this."

"That's what you like best about this place." He looked around them. "Everyone's always coming and going. You don't have to worry about them wanting to be with you for too long."

Maggie didn't reply. She didn't know what to say. She was too scared to offer him any assurances. She wasn't ready to commit her life to him. How could she know that these feelings wouldn't be gone tomorrow?

He got to his feet. "I have to get our things together. I'll email you some names and addresses of good accountants. I'll still finish the work on the fundraiser for you. It's the least I can do for all your trouble with Jordan."

"Adam?"

He didn't turn back to look at her. "Yes?"

"I'm sorry it can't be different."

"Me, too."

Delta found Maggie sitting in the chair in her office. "Do you understand the new system?"

"No."

"What are you doing with that tie?"

"Nothing."

"Maggie?"

"Don't say it!"

"I wouldn't know where to start anyway, honey. Our lives are just a mess, aren't they?"

Maggie spent the rest of the day thinking about calling Adam. She actually picked up the phone then set it back down. What would she say? *I was thinking about you. Maybe I want to have a relationship with you after all.*

He was right. She was a coward where those emotions were concerned. She didn't want to be sorry someday that she'd allowed herself to be put in that situation. Despite her feelings for him, Maggie was terrified of making a mistake. So she did what she'd always done: hoped that the feelings and the situation would go away. She kept herself busy and cried herself to sleep that night.

Adam's fundraising operation was in high gear. They were beginning to get phone calls from newspapers and television stations about the project. Questions and answers took up a lot of Maggie's time. It was billed as The Miracle House: Raising A New Roof for Small Miracles. Everyone seemed to be interested.

Delta brought in a flood of contributions from the mailbox. "We have *got* to find ourselves an accountant. I don't want you losing these."

"Delta, will you give it a rest?"

"And maybe it should be somebody who won't care about your no-relationship policy, huh? Maybe a nice, eighty-year-old married woman. Would that suit you?"

"Go away."

"Look at you," Delta pointed out. "You're miserable. He's miserable. What's the problem with trying it, honey? What have you got to lose? It might work. And if it doesn't, you're already miserable."

Maggie ignored her and picked up the checks. She dutifully put the amounts into the spreadsheet. She put the checks into one of the bank bags that Adam had provided for them to make deposits. "Could we change the subject? I know you don't want me to start asking questions about Dan."

"All right." Delta perched on the edge of the desk and changed the subject. "What are you wearing to the fundraiser?"

"I don't know."

"It's a costume party. This isn't something you can let creep up on you! It's only two weeks away. And don't even think you don't have to be there!"

"Okay." Maggie looked up at her. "What are you going to wear?"

"I'm going down to the costume shop today and renting my costume. Want me to rent one for you, too?"

"That would be great. Thanks."

"That's the Maggie I know and love!" Delta rumpled her hair. "I won't be gone long. Need anything while I'm out?"

"No, thanks."

"Don't work too hard now. Call an accountant!"

"I will," Maggie promised.

Lost in the process of trying to talk to any of the accountants Adam listed for her, Maggie heard the phone ring. She picked it up to hear Jordan crying on the other end. She hadn't seen the girl since Adam took her home two weeks ago. "What's wrong, Jordan?"

"My uncle is sending me away."

"You told him that's what you wanted. You made your point loud and clear."

"Maggie, I don't *really* want to go to Canada. You know that. I don't know anybody there. They talk funny. I want to stay here with my friends. My uncle—"

"—is doing what you said you wanted him to do. Have you told him you don't want to go?"

"Yes." Jordan sniffed. "He won't listen. He called my great-aunt this morning. He's taking me up there next week."

"I don't know what I can do, Jordan."

"You can talk to him, Maggie. He likes you. He'll listen to you."

"I don't think I can do that."

"Please, Maggie. I don't want to go away. I was wrong to say I did. I just wanted to get Uncle Adam's attention. I just wanted him to notice me for a change instead of his stupid business."

"I'll see what I can do." Maggie cut off her pleading. "I'm not promising anything."

"Thanks. You're great."

Maggie hung up the phone regretfully. She didn't want to see Adam right now. She didn't think he was going to listen to her. But she'd promised Jordan. She knew that Adam would regret sending the girl away. All of the shelter kids would be at school for the next two hours. She didn't have any excuse for not going to see him.

Even worse, she was excited at the prospect of seeing him. Everything had already been said between the two of them. Nothing had changed. But she wanted to hear his voice and look into his eyes. Even if it broke her heart.

Maggie pulled on her purple coat and zipped up her knee high black boots. She checked her hair and put on new lipstick. When she saw the wistful look in her eyes, she reminded herself that she was going to plead *Jordan's* case. Not her own. Then she set out in the bright sunshine for Adam's office.

She hesitated as she was about to knock on the Fuentes and Son-Sales door, but the sun was warm on her head and the sky was so blue. It was a day to believe in miracles. She grabbed what was left of her courage and knocked hard on the door.

"Yes?" He was wearing his black-rimmed glasses and holding a pen in one hand. "Oh. Hello, Maggie."

That deflated her bubble a little. He didn't sound happy to see her. "Hi, Adam."

He opened the door. "Is there a problem?"

"A small one." She stepped into the room. "Jordan called me."

He took a deep breath. Seeing her standing there, not being able to touch her, was nearly too much for him. He went back into his office. "I'm kind of busy right now, Maggie."

"You're sending her to Canada?"

"Yes. It's what Jordan wants to do. If she made it any clearer, she might be dead right now."

"She doesn't really want to go." Maggie paced the worn carpet with long strides. "She wants to stay here with you."

"I don't believe that."

"She called me and told me."

"It's another game." He tried to tune her out by concentrating on his work.

"The two of you have some problems. You can't throw away a chance for a wonderful relationship because you're afraid you can't find the answer!"

Adam stared at her with hungry, angry eyes. "Do you realize what you just said to me?"

Maggie played her words back in her head. "It's not the same."

He got up and walked close to her. "What's not the same?"

"You having a relationship with Jordan. Or—or with me." Standing beside him was making her head feel like a balloon. Her face was hot and her heart was racing. *Why did I agree to come? I can't even fight my own battles!*

"Glad you can see the analogy," he remarked sarcastically. "So many people are too pig-headed to see it."

"Adam—"

"Maggie?"

"We, uh, all have to make our choices. We have to pick

our battles." He was moving closer. His hand touched hers. She felt the impact like a fire rushing up her arm to her chest. He slid his free hand through a few strands of her hair.

He lowered his head towards her and whispered, "Even when the battles are the wrong ones?"

She knew he was going to kiss her. She surrendered gracefully to it. She closed her eyes and waited with her lips slightly parted. Her chest moved with her quick, shallow breaths. Anticipation thrilled through every pore in her body. *This is why I came. This is what I want.*

Adam looked at her and realized that he loved her. He loved the little freckles on her nose and the way her hair scattered around her head. He loved her sharp mind and her quick laugh. It stabbed him like a bolt of lightning, making his heart stop and miss a beat. He was terrified by the revelation. Then he was angry. *How can I love another woman who doesn't want me? It's not possible.* Without a word or another touch, he turned and walked away from her.

Maggie opened her eyes, closed her lips, and felt like a fool. "I guess I should be going," she said hesitantly. I told Jordan I'd talk to you. I wish you wouldn't send her away. She needs you. I think you're making a big mistake."

"That makes two of us."

She cleared her throat and walked to the door. "Good-bye, Adam."

He didn't reply. He wished he could tell her good-bye and never see her again. Was it too much to ask that he'd meet someone, *anyone*, who was crazy enough to love him in return?

Maggie rushed back to the shelter and ran upstairs to her room. She took a quick shower then looked at herself in the steamy mirror. There was an unhappy, tear-stained face looking back at her.

How did this happen to her in such a short amount of time? How was it possible that she came to care so much for Adam? And what did she think was going to happen when she went there? Did she think he was going to welcome her with open arms after she told him there was no place in her life for him?

Ruthlessly, she threw her wet towel into the dirty clothes hamper. She dried her hair and put on her clothes. She stormed downstairs in time for all of the kids to come home from school.

After dinner that night, she was logging checks into the computer spreadsheet again. The phone hadn't stopped ringing all day. They had interviews and donor visits lined up for every day until the fundraiser. Adam definitely had some contacts.

She shook her head and tried to refocus on her spreadsheet. *Adam's spreadsheet.* A few of his pens were still on her desk. She opened her desk drawer and looked at the tie she'd hidden in there. *Adam's tie*. She sighed then slammed the drawer shut. This wasn't going to get her anywhere! She knew they couldn't be together. She accepted that fact. What was her problem?

Delta knocked quickly on the door. "Maggie, come into the kitchen."

"What's up?"

"Kevin and Robbie are here."

Surprised, Maggie followed her. Even more surprising, she found Robbie and Kevin in the kitchen with Adam and Jordan. "What's going on?"

"Hear them out before you make up your mind," Adam suggested.

Robbie stepped forward "We were camping out under the Ninth Street Bridge. We saw Jazzy over there. Her mother left her again."

Maggie swore under her breath. "Why didn't she come back with you?"

"She wouldn't come. She said you'd only give her back to her mom again," Kevin told her.

"Besides, we weren't going to come back here to tell you after you threw us out," Robbie added. "We went to tell Jordan and Mr. Fuentes. They were the ones who brought us back."

"I have to go and talk to her," Maggie told Delta.

"I know. I'll hold down the fort here."

"She's out in the car," Jordan said. "We brought her here. She said she'd talk to you."

Maggie was amazed. She looked at Adam but there was no guessing what he was thinking.

Kevin and Robbie stood near the door. They looked downcast, rubbing their wet tennis shoes on the wooden floor.

Maggie relented. "I suppose I owe you something for bringing her in."

"Nah. You don't owe us nothin'."

"Maybe another chance?" Adam suggested.

Robbie brightened at once. "We could do it. Couldn't we, Kev?"

"We could," Kevin agreed. "We're different now."

"Yeah. We learned our lesson the hard, *cold* way. Give us another chance, Ms. Madison. Only one. We won't screw up this time."

Maggie looked at the two of them. She could feel the pressure of twenty other pairs of ears listening from around the corner. Every kid in the shelter would know what happened that night. Every kid on the street would know soon after. She glanced at Delta who nodded slightly. "All right. But this is it. Make sure you understand that. There won't be another chance after this one."

"Yes, ma'am."

Maggie nodded. "Let me get my coat."

"Thanks, Ms. Madison, Ms. Sommers."

"Don't thank me," Delta told them. "You're both gonna be on garbage detail for a month!"

Both of the boys were still grinning.

The Mercedes was running in the drive to keep it warm. Jazzy's pale little face looked out the window at Maggie as she walked outside with Jordan and Adam.

Maggie opened the door and climbed in beside her. "Jazzy, I want to help. Come inside and let's talk."

"Why? If my mom comes back, she'll know where to find me."

"We could stall her next time. Maybe even keep her from trying to get you back. She's abandoned you twice."

"It was her boyfriend, Chino." Jazzy made a face. "He's all she cares about now."

"Don't stay out on the street," Maggie said. "Come in with me."

"I heard you threw Kevin and Robbie out." Jazzy looked out of the window at Adam. "I guess you have your own man problems, huh?"

"Robbie and Kevin had their own problems. They didn't have anything to do with me." Maggie held out her hand. "Come in with me?"

Jazzy nodded. "Okay. For now anyway. But I don't want to go back to school."

"You know the rules."

"*You* came out here to get *me*," Jazzy reminded her. "I don't have to go in with you."

"You're right. You could stay out in the cold under the bridge. That sounds like fun. If that's what you want." Maggie opened her door and started to get out of the car.

Jazzy only waited a minute to see if she was sincere. "Wait!"

Maggie turned back to face her with a sigh of relief. "You'll still have to go to school. It's the only way to make sure this doesn't happen to you as an adult."

"I can do that."

Maggie hugged her. "Let's go inside, huh?"

Adam was waiting at the door. "I'm glad you found her. And I'm glad you let Robbie and Kevin come back."

She turned to him as Jazzy was going inside. Jordan was already getting in the car. "Thanks for bringing her back."

"Sure."

Maggie watched him walk to his car. She wanted to say something to him. "Adam?"

"Yes?"

Words came and went through her mind like a flock of birds. *Don't leave. Let's work this out. There must be something we can do.* None of them would come out of her mouth. "Drive safely."

He didn't reply. Maggie watched him drive away until she couldn't see the red taillights on his car in the darkness. She went inside slowly. Delta had disappeared upstairs.

There was a knock at the door as she turned out the lights. She looked out of the window. Brewster Madison stood in a circle of light on the back step.

Her heart froze even as she panicked. How many times when she was a child had she prayed to look out her aunt's door and see him standing there? All those years of yearning and loneliness flooded through her. She closed her eyes and rested her head against the doorframe. *Why now?*

Adam had defended her father's actions. The hurt and bitter child in her whispered, "excuses." She didn't know if she could find it in her to talk to him. She knew she could never forgive him.

He knocked on the door and she jumped. But she didn't answer. She wanted to pretend that she didn't hear him. Maybe he'd go away. Maybe he'd never try and see her again. She waited, barely breathing in the warm kitchen. The night outside the door was cold and empty.

When she peeked out the window again, he was walking away. A terrible realization seized her. Adam was right. If she didn't try to let her father make amends, she might never know the man her mother loved. A few weeks ago, she would've turned away. But that was before Adam made her question everything about her life. Tonight, she opened the door and ran outside. "Wait!"

"Maggie?" Brewster Madison turned back to look at her. "You know, you look just like your mama."

She didn't know what to call him so she skipped past that detail. "Would you like to come in and have some coffee?"

His face broke into a wreath of smiles. "I've waited my whole life to hear you say that, darlin'."

Maggie's hand shook as she poured coffee for both of them. She couldn't believe that her father was sitting in her kitchen. She studied him surreptitiously.

It had been too dark in the coffeehouse to really get a look at his face. He looked much different than she imagined he would. He was older, for one thing. Or maybe a hard life had left him looking old and haggard. He had a raspy voice that suited his music. There was acceptance and humor in his dark eyes.

"I know this must be kind of weird for you." Brewster shifted nervously in his chair.

She sat down opposite him at the long table. Tongue-tied and awkward, she searched for something to say to him. Words failed her. What could she say to him? He was the epitome of everything wrong in her world for as long as she could remember. He was a stranger. Yet, there was something so familiar about him that she felt she'd know him anywhere.

Brewster seemed to understand her dilemma. He began speaking in his deep, throaty voice. "You know, when your mama died, I didn't know what to do. I had this sweet little girl who was heartbroken because her mama left her. Everything I did seemed to be wrong."

"So you left me with Aunt Leila." Maggie found her voice.

He sipped his coffee. "Yes, I did. I wasn't much good back then at earning a living with my music. I wanted you to have everything. But more than that, I thought Leila could give you what you needed emotionally. What did I know about raising a little girl?"

"I understand that. But why didn't you want *any* part of my life?" The voice of the hurt little girl echoed in Maggie's words. "Why didn't you ever call or write or something? I looked for you on every birthday. I used to wait by the mailbox for some word from you. I stared out of the front windows of Aunt Leila's house waiting for you to come back for me."

His lined, weary face was bleak. "I never knew. But I did call and write. After a while, I thought you hated me because you never answered back. I talked to your aunt. She told me she never gave you my letters or told you that I called. She said it would be too confusing for you, that she couldn't raise you if I interfered. I didn't question her on what was right for you. I thought she knew best. But I always sent a present for you on your birthday and at Christmas. I guess she thought it was best not to give you those either."

Maggie wished she couldn't imagine her aunt saying or doing those things. But Aunt Leila was an absolute ruler. She had definite opinions on the way everything should be done. There was her way and the wrong way. She knew her aunt loved her. It was easier to blame her father. Until that night at the coffeehouse, he had been a faceless stranger.

"Leila did a good job. Just look at you!" Brewster looked down into his coffee cup. "I know you must hate me. And I know I'm as much to blame as Leila by not staying put and working in the mill or something. My music was all I ever had. When your mama told me she loved me, I wanted to change. She told me that my music was my gift to the world. I did the best I could. I know it wasn't enough."

Maggie closed her eyes. She couldn't actually remember her mother's face. All she knew about her was from pictures and what her aunt told her. She didn't know this man. But she knew her Aunt Leila. Sad to say, his words held a ring of truth.

"I'm not asking you to forgive me for all those years," Brewster said. "I was just hoping we might be able to meet. Just sitting down here with you is a gift for me."

"I wish I would've known," she reflected. "You're right. I've spent my whole life hating you for not wanting me. It created all of this." She glanced around the quiet shelter. "I wanted to help other kids who felt like I felt."

"Then you did something good with it." Brewster smiled at her. "I'm sorry I let Leila talk me out of what was right. I'm sorry I couldn't be there for you. But I've always loved you, Maggie. You'll always be my little girl."

Her throat constricted. "I don't know what to say. I don't think I can change the way I feel just because I've met you. What I feel is so much a part of who I am. I don't know if I can let that go."

He nodded and shuffled to his feet. "I understand. Well, it was nice meeting you. Thanks for the coffee."

Maggie stood up quickly and took his hand. His fingers were rough and calloused. Musician's hands. "But I'm willing to give it some time if you are."

His smile created a warm light in his face. "When I saw you at the coffeehouse the other night with your friend, I knew it was a sign from heaven. Looking at you was like looking into the face of an angel. Your mama's eyes. Your mama's smile. I've got all the time in the world, darlin'. You just let me know how you want to play it."

Then Maggie did something she'd never imagined herself doing. She hugged her father. "Thanks." She wiped tears from her eyes. "You know I might have mama's eyes and smile. But I think I got your nose and ears."

His big arms came around her and held her tight. "Poor baby. Good thing you can have long hair to hide those satellite dishes the Creator gave us! That would be enough to make you hate me."

"I don't think so," Maggie told him. "I can hear a kid sneaking around in this big old house even with a pillow over my head."

Brewster laughed. "Well, that's a blessing too then."

Delta tiptoed into the brightly lit kitchen. "Is everything okay down here?"

Maggie moved away from her father. "Delta, I'd like you to meet someone."

"Okay." Delta's dark eyes flitted between her partner and the husky man standing beside her. "What's up?"

"Brewster Madison, this is my partner, Delta Sommers. Delta, this is my father."

Brewster stepped forward and shook Delta's hand. "Pleased to meet you, ma'am."

Delta's smile lit up her face. "Well, I am pleased to make your acquaintance, Mr. Madison. Your daughter is a wonderful woman."

"Please call me Brewster. Nobody's called me Mr. Madison in forty years."

They all had another cup of coffee. The conversation was light and didn't linger on anything that had happened in the past. Dan joined them after bringing in another runaway. Delta got the boy settled while Maggie did the paperwork at the table by her father. They sat and talked after that until daylight was beginning to etch the dark sky in gold and pink.

Brewster left after hugging Maggie and Delta. He promised to stay in touch and invited them down to his newly bought jazz club.

Delta took the coffee cups to the sink after he was gone. "You know, Maggie, you had me worried when I first came into the kitchen."

"Why's that?" Maggie asked her as she ran water into the sink.

"When I saw you hugging that man, I thought you went out and found a replacement for Adam in your life." Delta shrugged. "He looked like a carpenter to me. And you know how you are with those service men."

Dan laughed. "And on that note, I have to get going. See you tonight, sweetie?"

Delta nodded and kissed him. "You know it. I've got a thing for policemen like stick-girl has a thing for people who fix things."

Maggie sighed and dumped pancake mix into a big bowl. She could already hear children upstairs getting ready for school. It was going to be a long day.

Chapter Twelve

There was a press conferencc a week later. CNN and all the local television stations were at the shelter. The weather was still cold. But warm sunlight bathed the Small Miracles Shelter in a golden light.

Maggie looked out the window as Delta fussed with her flowered dress. Cameras were everywhere. People milled on their small lawn and in the street where the cops kept traffic back. This was the official kick off of the fundraiser. Delta had put balloons everywhere around the house. They waved colorfully in the breeze.

"How do I look?" Delta asked her.

"You look fine."

"Maggie? Could I have your attention for one tiny moment? I'm about to go live in front of twenty million viewers. I'd like an *honest* opinion!"

Maggie turned back to her. "You look great. What's not to love? You always look good in flowers."

Delta looked in the mirror and pursed her lips. "Do you like this shade of lipstick?"

"Sure." Maggie had already turned back to look out the window again.

"Do you see him yet?"

"Who?"

"Like you don't know who I'm talking about! The man

who's had you wandering the house every night and looking more stick-girl than ever, that's *who!*"

"If you mean Adam," Maggie responded, "I don't see him. But I don't wander the house every night and I haven't lost any weight. This was *my* decision, Delta. It's not like he threw me over. I'm not pining away for him."

"Sure. Whatever you say, honey. You just sit there and be stubborn and you'll spend your whole life looking out that window while life passes you by."

"I don't think life is passing me by. Will you leave it alone, please?"

"Whatever you say." Delta shook her head.

"You keep saying that."

"I'm not arguing with you."

"Good."

Delta looked at herself in the mirror again. "This dress makes my hips look *huge!* With those cameras adding ten pounds, I wish I had your stick-girl body today."

Maggie sighed. "You look fine. They're here to see the shelter, not us."

"Is that why you look like a rutabaga?"

"I don't look like a rutabaga!"

There was a knock on the door as Delta was about to argue her point.

"Delta? Maggie?"

It was Adam.

Maggie wanted to run and hide. She knew he was coming. She knew she was going to have to see him, speak to him. She wasn't prepared for the onslaught of emotion that filled her when he walked into the room. Her knees were weak. She couldn't speak. *This isn't happening to me! I can't be in love with Adam Fuentes.*

Was he always so handsome? Does the curve in his bottom lip really fit mine as well as I remember? Why does his gaze make me feel like I've had too much to drink?

"Adam! How do I look?" Delta grabbed him and made him look at her.

"You look great! Like a spring day!"

"Are you sure? Because stick-girl over here won't do anything but look out the window!"

Adam looked at Maggie. "Nervous?"

"No."

"It'll be over pretty quickly. The mayor will speak then he'll turn the microphone over to the two of you. No one expects you to give a speech. Just say a few words about the shelter."

"That's fine." Maggie's words were faint. Maggie *felt* faint.

"Will you be there, honey?" Delta asked him. " 'Cause I'll feel a lot better seeing your handsome face in that crowd."

Adam laughed. "I'll be there. But I don't think you'll have any trouble. I haven't seen a time either one of you were at a loss for words."

"I was just telling stick-girl here that she looks like a rutabaga. What do you think?"

He was trying *really* hard not to notice what Maggie looked like. Or that she was there at all. He'd managed to control his constant need to call her or see her. He didn't stand outside her door at night. It hadn't been easy.

Now he looked at her in her golden wool dress that barely reached her thighs. Her yellow tights showed the curves of her pretty legs. He swallowed hard. "She looks fine too."

"If you say so." Delta wasn't convinced.

Maggie smiled and pushed at her hair. "Thanks."

Adam continued to look at her. He memorized every curve of her cheek, every golden light in her hair. He remembered too well how she felt in his arms; how soft her lips were against his.

"We're ready when you are," Delta said, breaking up the staring match between them.

"Right." Adam gathered his crazy thoughts first. "Let's go."

The announcements were brief. The mayor promised to be back for the fundraiser and challenged the public to make this miracle come true. He shook hands with Delta who said a few words about how the shelter had changed her life. Then Delta stepped down and motioned for Maggie to say something.

Maggie took her friend's place at the podium. She looked out at the crowd. It all narrowed down to Adam's face. "I'd just like to say thank you to Adam Fuentes for making all of this possible. The children of Atlanta, *all of the children*, deserve the best we can give them. Thanks for your help."

Applause burst out in the crowd. The mayor made the rounds shaking hands and having pictures taken. Well-wishers and reporters cornered Maggie. When the crowds began to die away, she looked up and found Adam standing beside her.

"Hi. Thanks for coming." *She still sounded like she was talking to a stranger.* "Really. Delta was right. It was nice to see your face in the crowd. And I meant what I said about you helping us with this."

"I was glad to help, Maggie. You know that." He glanced at his watch.

"Will you be here for the fundraiser?"

"I'll be back from Vancouver the night before."

"You're taking Jordan away then?"

"There's not much reason to talk about this anymore. It's going to happen."

"I understand."

He looked at his watch again.

"Well, I've got to go." She lied to save them both from the awkward moment. *I love you. I love you. I love you.*

"Me, too. You both did a great job. I'll see you next week."

"Yeah."

Delta came to stand beside Maggie as she watched Adam walk away. "You are pathetic, child. You know that, don't you?"

"It's even worse than you know."

"Hello, Delta." Dan nodded to her. "Maggie, you looked good up there."

Maggie smiled. "Thanks, Dan. How's it going?"

He shrugged his broad shoulders. "It's going."

Delta glanced up and smiled at Dan. Maggie made an excuse to leave them alone. She wasn't really sure if they heard her.

The day of the fundraiser dawned bright, clear, and warm. The blue sky stretched on endlessly with no hint of rain in the forecast. Adam looked up toward the sky and smiled. It was perfect. He watched the kids running through the spring green grass in the park.

There was already a good crowd gathered there. It looked like the invitations he sent to community leaders and potential donors were well received. The media picked up on the event with gusto. There were satellite trucks from all the major networks. He couldn't ask for more.

Multi-colored balloons were tethered to signs for the fundraiser event. They rivaled the season's first red and yellow tulips in their jewel tones. The park itself was cooperating with the plan. Dogwood trees were blossoming and birds called from the branches of the greening oak trees.

He walked through the crowd and checked on everything that was being set up. The mayor and his guests at the podium were adjusting the microphones for their speeches. Adam's pirate costume, complete with eye patch and sword, seemed ridiculous at the store. Then he saw the mayor dressed as a clown with huge floppy red shoes. He didn't feel so bad.

He checked with a few speakers and made sure the program line-up was right. All of the Atlanta newspapers and television stations were there along with a few reporters from the national media. The mayor shook his hand and proclaimed the fundraiser an excellent idea. All the time, Adam's eyes were searching the faces for the only one his heart wanted to see that day: Maggie. He didn't see her anywhere. *Where was she?*

He caught sight of Jasmine in a group near the fountain.

He cut his way politely through the people between them and hailed the girl. She would know where Maggie was.

She looked up at him. Her little face was sprinkled with glitter. "Hi, Mr. Fuentes! Is Jordan with you?"

"No. I like your costume."

"Thanks. Ms. Madison said I was a fairy princess. But I think I look more like an angel."

"You're a beautiful angel," he said, touching her chin. "Have you, uh, seen, Ms. Madison since you got here?"

Jazzy laughed. "Of course I've seen her! We came together. She was over there, by the big gold cup, with Ms. Sommers."

Adam scanned the area where Jasmine pointed. He couldn't tell if Maggie was there or not. Whose dumb idea was it to make this a costume party anyway? He seemed to recall that it was *his* idea, but that didn't make it any better.

He thanked the girl for her help. Then he began weaving his way through the crowd towards the golden donation cup. He didn't see Delta or Maggie close to the bandstand. It might help if he had some idea of what kind of costume Maggie was wearing. He should've thought to ask Jazzy.

An announcement from the bandstand cut through his thoughts. "And now, The Great Little Jazz Band." Applause sprinkled through the crowd.

Adam looked around. *That was Maggie's father's band.* He didn't hire them to be there. Did Maggie know? He looked for her again but still couldn't find her. Not that it mattered. She'd made her position clear. If she had feelings for him, she wasn't willing to share them. Even if she thought that he hired her father, what harm could it do?

Brewster Madison came to the microphone. "Thank you all. I'd like to dedicate this next song to my daughter, Maggie."

Adam finally saw Delta's face and made a straight line through the crowd towards her. Dan was standing beside her, his arm around her waist. He was dressed to look like W.C. Fields.

"Well, you look good." Delta greeted Adam. "Is this your true nature?"

"Thanks. I'm not sure anymore. Where's Maggie?"

"No chit chat? No *pretending* that you came to speak to me?" Delta pouted. "The least you could do is try to flatter the information out of me."

"Delta?"

"Sorry, honey." She patted the flowers on her bright red hat that matched her Mae West costume. "She's around here somewhere. I haven't seen her for a few minutes."

"Somewhere?" Adam was getting impatient. He wasn't sure why. Nothing had changed.

"You know Maggie. She could be anywhere."

"Did she come with you?"

"Oh, yeah!" Delta grinned broadly. "In that fine new bus that City Chevrolet donated to us last week. They even airbrushed *Small Miracles* on the side. It carries fifty kids! We think we should be able to take care of that many in the new shelter, thanks to you."

Adam smiled, distracted. "You know I was glad to help."

"How's Jordan?"

"She's fine. She's with her great-aunt in Vancouver. Did Maggie say anything about the band playing today?"

Delta frowned. "No. What was she supposed to say?"

"I don't know. I have to find her."

"I don't know where Maggie got off to, Adam, but she's here somewhere." She patted his shoulder. "Slow down, sugar. You're going to have a heart attack if you keep on this way."

"Thanks." Adam nodded to Dan. "Nice costume."

Dan smiled. "You too, man. What we do for these ladies, huh?"

Adam shook his head then left them. He renewed his efforts to find Maggie as the sounds of her father's jazz band filtered through the trees around him.

He told himself that he only wanted to find her to explain that he didn't hire her father. He knew it was a lie. But it was a plausible one. It would be something to say to her when he found her. Maybe he wouldn't sound so pathetic. *I was only looking for you to explain about your father . . .*

It didn't have anything to do with how much he missed her. Or how much he loved her and wished she'd reconsider. After not seeing her for so long, he knew he'd take any bone she threw him. She didn't have to love him in return. Maybe if he agreed to donate money or supplies on a regular basis, she'd agree to see him. Even if it was only to thank him.

After searching for Maggie for half an hour and not finding her, Adam felt like he finally understood. She didn't want him to find her. Despite the size of the crowd, he managed to find everyone else from the shelter. Maggie had neatly avoided him. He was tired from his flight back from Canada. He'd driven straight over from the airport. He covered all of the bases for the fundraiser. It was time to go home.

It was probably for the best that he didn't see her anyway. Talking to her about her father seemed a little contrived. The one thing he couldn't handle was her pity. If he kept his distance, his heart would always long for her. It would be painful but not as bad as if she told him they could only be friends. He took off his sword and threw it into the backseat of the Mercedes. He changed his mind about going home and headed for his office.

He barely sat down to work when there was a knock at the door. He looked down at his costume. He didn't care if someone saw him in it, but he *did* pull off the eye patch. He yanked open the door with an impatient hand. "Yes?"

"Good morning, Mr. Fuentes."

Adam took off his glasses and stared at her. He couldn't believe she was standing there. "Ms. Madison."

"It's a beautiful morning, isn't it?"

"Yes. It is."

"I'm here . . ."

". . . about the shelter?"

Maggie looked into his beautiful golden eyes and swallowed hard. She'd followed him home from the park to tell him. It had taken a few minutes in the car to build up the nerve. She'd rehearsed it over and over again in her mind. She knew what she wanted to say. She just didn't know how to say it. "Well, yes and no."

"Oh?" He stood in the doorway with the door open halfway. She wasn't in costume after all. Unless you considered the very short, very tight, almost indecent black dress a costume. The hem couldn't be much below her . . .

"Can I come in?" She hoped he wouldn't turn her away. She didn't miss his interested perusal of her dress. Maybe that was enough to make him listen to what she had to say. If that was the best she could get from him right now, she supposed it was what she deserved.

Adam saw a pair of construction workers looking at her from across the street. One of them whistled loudly. He started to yell at the men then changed his mind. He opened the door wide instead. "I think you should."

Maggie laughed at the whistle. "Ignore them. Charlie's just a tease."

Adam closed the door and leaned against it. "Maggie, what can you expect? In that dress, you look—"

"Yes?" She sat down on the brown chair near the door. She wanted to cross her legs and bat her eyelashes but this was as seductive as she knew how to get. Even with practice. Delta had a few pointers but Maggie couldn't go through with them.

Adam couldn't ignore her. His eyes moved up her legs from the black heels to the short skirt like a hungry man eyes a pastry. He shook his head and walked past her into the other office. What did she want from him? He didn't know if he was coming or going anymore. He hid his heart in gruff sarcasm. "Is this a new game, Maggie? I'm kind of busy right now. Shouldn't you be at the fundraiser?"

"Shouldn't *you* be there?" She jumped up from the chair and followed him into his office. She'd thought about this too long to let him go that easily. He wasn't going to ignore her today. One way or another, she was going to say what she came to say.

"I checked in." He tried not to look at her. "Everything was fine. There wasn't any reason for me to stay."

She looked at his costume, wishing she was daring enough to touch him. "You look cute."

"Maggie," he ground out, wanting to snap his pencil in half, "what do you want from me?"

A beautiful dress doesn't do any good if you stand against the wall at the party. Maggie remembered reading that in a magazine when she was a teenager. She squared her shoulders and went to sit on his desk beside him. "I came here to talk to you."

Was she deliberately trying his patience . . . and his resistance? "I think we've said everything there is to say, don't you?"

She locked her gaze with his. "No. There's a world of things I haven't said. For starters," she swallowed hard, "I've missed you, Adam. I wish that we could try again."

He clenched a notebook until his knuckles turned white. "I'm really busy and I don't have time to play these games with you."

"This isn't a game!" She jumped up from the desk and paced the floor. "I believed that relationships were impossible for a really long time. It took me a while to realize that, with the right person, a relationship could be a good thing. And that not everyone leaves. You didn't desert Jordan. I wouldn't desert you."

"Do you realize what you're saying? I don't think I can handle an on-again/off-again thing with you, Maggie."

"I think so." She smiled weakly before coming to stand beside him. "I, at least, promise to give it my best. If you'll have me."

Adam kissed her before she could continue. He pressed her back against the big old desk, scattering every neat stack of paper to the floor. The phone fell with a ring and a thud. "Does that answer your question?"

"Oh, Adam, I've missed you." Tears spilled down her cheeks as she kissed him and held him to her with fierce determination. "I was such an idiot. Why didn't you just tell me? Since when have you had problems laying it on the line for me?"

"Yes," he agreed, kissing her throat and face, "you were an idiot. But what was I going to say? It doesn't always work out happily ever after, sweetheart. I wish it did." The little black dress conveniently slipped down off of one of her shoulders. "I *love* this dress. We need to buy you ten more like it."

"I thought you didn't like it? At the door—"

"You can't ever wear it outside. But you can wear it for me anytime." He sat back down in his big chair and brought her with him to snuggle into his lap. "Why are you *really* here?"

She smiled at him. "I thought it was obvious. I've been miserable and unhappy without you. I don't want to live that way anymore if I can help it. I thought this might be my only way to explain without having to go through all the stupid things I said to you."

"No problem." He played with the straps on her dress. "You got what you wanted. Where are we now?"

"Wherever you want to be."

Adam was hurt enough to be cautious. "What's changed, Maggie? Why do you feel so differently now?"

"I changed," she whispered. "You were right. There has to be something we can work out together. I've missed you so much. I'm so sorry I sent you away."

Adam hugged her closer. "I love you, Maggie. I love everything about you. I don't care if we argue or if you drag home every stray you find. I don't care if you don't want a relationship. I don't care about either of our pasts. I just want to be with you. I want to watch you wake up every morning and go to sleep with you every night."

She smiled and sniffed, wiping at her tears. "Well, I've decided that I want it all, so I hope you're serious. I want the ring and the white dress and dinner in front of the TV every night. I don't care if we're both miserable. I want us to be together."

"Maggie, I—"

"You did this to me."

"I did?"

"I was perfectly happy in my own little life. You changed all of that. I kept taking down walls for you."

He laughed. "*Me?* You kept knocking on *my* door, sweetheart. I couldn't look away forever."

"What about Jordan?"

He kissed her nose. "When Jordan and I were flying to Vancouver, we had a chance to talk. *Really talk* for the first time in a long time. We decided we wanted to be together. She's staying with her great-aunt for a while but then she's coming home. She's going to come to work with me here. Like I did with my father. And you were right. I don't have to work so hard. I was only doing it to protect myself. I have to make time in my life for her. *And* for you."

"That's so wonderful." She kissed him. "I'm so happy for you. I hope Jordan will be happy with the idea of you and I being together."

"Like you said, we'll work it out. Besides, didn't you tell me that it might be good for her? And she really likes you." He hugged her close, almost afraid to let her go. "Maggie, I saw your father at the park. I didn't have anything to do with him being there. I'm not sure how it happened, but I wouldn't do something like that to you."

"I know." She sighed. "It was part of what changed everything for me. I talked with him right after you left. He tried to see me, Adam, when I was a child. He sent me letters that my aunt didn't give me. He didn't completely desert me like I thought. All those years that were wasted for us. That's what made me decide that you and I couldn't make that mistake."

Adam smiled and nuzzled his face against her soft hair. "I don't really know your father, but I like him already. I'm glad that you're going to have him back in your life, Maggie. I'm glad that I'm going to keep Jordan in my life too."

"Is this where you ask me to marry you?" she prompted.

"I'd prefer to do this the old-fashioned way, if you don't

mind," he replied. "This isn't the same thing as pestering me to give money to the shelter!"

"That will be perfect too, won't it?" She grinned. "Your checkbook in my pocket!"

"I haven't even asked you yet!"

"You see? We could have saved all this confusion if you'd already taken care of it. Honestly, Adam, I—"

He kissed her fiercely until she was silent, then looked into her eyes. "Will you marry me . . . and my checkbook, Maggie Madison? Frozen food, runaway daughter, and all?"

She laughed. "Yes, Adam. I love you and I'll marry you. And considering that you're marrying Delta, fifty street kids and a jazz musician along with me, I think we're both getting a pretty good bargain!"